Chapter 1

I never thought I would be the sor

I suppose, to me, at least, death was the end of life and anything that lay beneath the cakey soil under my mud-soaked court shoes, was just fossilised earth.

But this was my father.

"Suzanna?"

I jumped, turning my head a fraction to the right. The flight had left me exhausted and I could barely lift my head to acknowledge my mother, now standing next to me. "We better be going, sweetheart. They'll all be waiting for us."

I could smell my mother's perfume – Gucci, of course – mingling with the rising scent of dew in the air and I swallowed back my distaste. I had barely had the energy to dress myself this morning, my grief threatening to eat me from the inside. And yet, here was my mother, dressed to the nines as if this was just another one of her cases.

"Could I, *please*, just have a few more minutes?" I spoke through gritted teeth, the effort hurting my jaw. I couldn't even lift my head high enough to meet her eye. "This is my last day with him."

The gentle song of a robin somewhere above me drowned out what I knew was my mother sighing in concentrated frustration.

"Of course, sweetheart." Her hand on my arm barely made contact, as if I was made of glass, too fragile to touch.
"I'll be waiting in the car."

With the sound of her footsteps receding, her yellow kitten heels piercing holes into the soft earth with each step, I drew in a deep breath through my nose. The cool Irish air settled in my lungs, blanketing my pain for a few moments before I felt the tears betray me.

Without another thought, I sank to the ground in the middle of Shanganagh Cemetery. I didn't care that I could feel the wet dew soaking through my sheer tights, the moss green colour I knew would be staining my knees by the second. My tears fell like rain into the earth where my father lay, one after another; a heavy downpour of long-buried memories and regret.

"I'm sorry I wasn't here…" I gulped air into my lungs, struggling for breath as I leant my palms against the soaked earth. "Life isn't fair, sometimes, is it? You always taught me that.."

I stood up, too quickly, and my head rushed. Steadying myself against the cool, marble headstone, I closed my eyes and felt the world spin against my blackened lids.

As I turned on my heel and made my way back across the expanse of dewy grass and stolen lives, I shook away the remains of my grief the best that I could and made my way to the car.

No one else would see me mourn today.

"Suzanna! What have you done to your tights?"

I carried on staring out of the car window, deliberately ignoring my mother's pettiness. I heard the familiar sigh of irritation escape her heavily made-up lips and I was amazed at how the exaggerated sound made me want to scream.

"Really, Suzanna! Stop acting like a child and look at me!"

For the first time since seeing my father laid to rest, I turned to look at my mother. Her golden blonde hair - reminiscent of 'The Rachel', circa 1994 – fell to her shoulders, setting off baby blue eyes that no one could deny were the mirror of my own. It was one of the only things that I liked about my appearance, and probably the only thing I was thankful to my mother for.

My eyes got me noticed. And I don't mean to say that arrogantly, they really did. When I was five years old, a talent scout spotted me on the street while shopping with my mother and suggested I come to their studio for a photoshoot. Much to my mother's dismay, I didn't receive a call-back - a reason she now puts down to my 'au naturale' use of make-up that I now adopt.

I stared at her now, pursing her lips that were a richly applied coral colour, and I suddenly realised that I couldn't remember the last time my mother had spoken to me so sharply. It disturbed me, just slightly.

"Look, sweetheart", she lowered her voice, suddenly aware that the driver was staring at us both worriedly through the rear-view mirror. Fleetingly, I felt his pain, having to endure such a tense car-ride home. I almost made myself smile, then. "I understand, this is a difficult day for both of us…"

"What do you understand, Mum?" She stared through me, then, not at me, and I steadied myself against the force of her gaze. "You go back home to your own perfect life, to Graham, to your big house in the country. And what do I have to go back to? A job that barely pays my rent, memories of a man that screwed me around and left me to pick up the pieces?"

I had stunned her, I could tell. Her eyes were wide on mine, with just a tint of compassion softening her perfect features. Only a tint, though. The rest of her gaze was focussed on not giving away the obvious disappointment that her only daughter thought so little of her.

"Suzanna, I…"

"I don't feel like talking anymore."

I turned back to face the car window, staring out at tree after tree, and almost making myself cross-eyed in the process.

As the driver turned right onto the long gravel driveway of 206 Aintree House, I was sure that I heard a shuddering exhalation next to me that almost sounded like sorrow.

It had always baffled me as to why my mother had chosen Graham Connors as her second choice. Or maybe he was her third or fourth? I had lost count after the first betrayal.

Of course, Graham had money. The house itself stood for that fact. I opened the car door and was greeted by the heady scent of lavender and honeysuckle in the air. Walking around the side of the car to the front of the house, I noticed the ivy hugging the perimeter of the huge house, climbing the copper-bricked walls as if desperately trying to escape. I felt their pain, I thought, with a wry smile.

"Come on, sweetheart." My mother waited for me by the huge oak door, shielded beneath an even bigger alcove that held a various array of hanging baskets. The mix of floral scents that filled the alcove almost made me gag. "Everyone's waiting."

I took her hand, albeit reluctantly, and let her lead me across the threshold of her home. When I stepped into the hall, I instantly felt like I had stepped through a portal into another dimension. It was so quiet outside, the Irish air cool and calming compared to what now greeted me. Inside, it was sticky and humid and full of faces that carried the same expression, as each one assessed me individually.

"Oh, pet, come here!"

A short, rotund woman with curls of carrot-coloured hair took a step towards me, chubby arms extended out. Her bottom lip was stuck out, almost comically, in a show of sympathy and I tried my best to hide my disdain.

I forced a grateful smile at her show of concern and let her put her arms around me. She practically squeezed the blood from my veins with her bulky body and I met my mother's eye from the corner of my own. I noticed she was trying to hide a smile and I couldn't help but chuckle a little inside myself.

When the ginger-haired woman eventually pulled me free, I let out a heavy breath of relief and looked into her round, saucer-like eyes. "Now you tell me if you need anything, won't you, pet? I'm just a few streets down! I can be at your door in the blink of an eye, I can!"

I need my father, I thought, as if I was nothing more than a child having a silent tantrum. But, of course, I didn't say that.

"Thank you." I didn't even know the woman's name. I tried to catch my mother's eye but she was standing by the spiral staircase, deep in conversation with an elderly couple. I turned back to the carrot-topped lady. "But I don't actually live around here. I moved to a little town in Cornwall a few years back now. Mousehole, in Penzance. Do you know it?"

I was trying my best to make conversation but I could see by the woman's expression that my words had not registered in her mind at all.

"Oh, I'm afraid not, pet!" Her laugh was throaty, and I assumed that she must have been a smoker. "I don't travel much out of Foxrock! Me and Jim like to stay close to home, don't we, my dear?"

As if from nowhere, an even shorter man appeared from behind the rotund woman and gave his wife a broad smile.

"What's that you're sayin', love?" He was clasping a half-empty pint of Guinness in his hand and had florid red cheeks. I assumed that wasn't his first pint.

Before his wife could roll off another spiel of questions my way, I took my chance. "I hope you don't mind, but I'm just going to make myself a drink..."

The woman appraised me fleetingly, as if she had forgotten my presence altogether and I was silently relieved.

"Of course, pet. You do as you please!" She patted my arm, a little condescendingly, I thought, and I made my way over to the kitchen at the end of the hall.

The kitchen seemed bigger to me than the last time I had been here and I marvelled at the huge bay window in front of me that looked out over the well-manicured gardens. Remembering where Mum kept the glasses, I poured myself a Rosé, dismissing the little voice in my head that told me it's too early to start drinking.

"Little early for that, isn't it, Suze?"

Just when I thought I was going crazy, I turned around to see a familiar face. I nearly choked on my drink. "Kevlar?!"

Kevin Brady grinned at me - my reference to many episodes of Gavin and Stacey spiralling back to our minds in an instant - and, immediately, I was transported back nearly ten years to my youth; sitting on my fathers worn, old sofa, a bottle of Corona in my hand as we put the world to rights in just a few hours.

"And it's still Boozy Suzy, I see?"

He nodded towards my wine glass and I couldn't help but laugh for old times' sake. "Hey, this is a one-off, alright? And I think I have an excuse, don't you?"

I had meant it in light-hearted humour given the recent events of the day, but my heart did an odd sort of flip when Kevin put his hand on my arm. His touch was so uncharacteristically tender that it threw me, if only for a moment.

"How are you doing, Suze?"

Kevin stared at me, his gaze fixed on mine and I couldn't help but notice how handsome he had become. He had seemed so young the last time I had seen him that I almost didn't recognise the boy – no, man – now standing in front of me.

His thick, chestnut brown hair curled around his ears and across his forehead, and his eyes had seemed to turn from a youthful blue to a sort of blueish-green. Not too dissimilar to the colour of the ocean just outside my own front door in Mousehole.

"I'm…" I struggled for the right words, still feeling Kevin's touch on my arm. "I'm coping."

He smiled sympathetically, the same way everyone else had done the moment I stepped through the front door and found myself resenting him for it under my breath.

"You know, Suze…" He lowered his head coyly, and I wondered what was going through his head. "I always used to have a crush on you when we were friends!" My mouth dropped open almost instantaneously. "Oh, come on!" Kevin blushed like a teenager and rolled his head to one side, as if too afraid now to meet my gaze. "You must have known! I was a horny seventeen-year old kid!"

I laughed, loud enough for a few people in the hall to look up from their polite conversations, surprised at who could possibly be having so much fun in the midst of such a sombre occasion. Quite frankly, I didn't care what they thought.

"So, you're saying I was just another one of your page three's?"

He blushed even more violently then, a similar shade to my drink, and immediately, I realised my mistake.

"You know what?" I turned to put my drink down, blushing violently myself. "I don't want to know!"

We both laughed then as a voice called down from the hallway.

"Kevin? There you are!" A petite woman with dark, brown curls entered in a flurry. Her pretty brown eyes looked racked with exhaustion and I noticed, with a surprising jolt, that she was heavily pregnant. "I've been looking all over for..."

When she noticed me standing in front of her, the young woman's stern expression soon dissolved into something resembling pity.

"Hey, Suzanna." Her voice oozed false sympathy. "I'm so sorry for your loss."

I forced on the smile I had been practicing all morning. "Thank you. Um, I'm sorry, I don't believe I know..."

"Sorry, Suze!" Kevin put an arm around the pretty young woman. "This is Alana, my wife."

For the second time that day, my mouth dropped open.

"You're married? But you're just a squirt!"

Kevin and I laughed in unison. Alana, meanwhile, remained silent by her husband's side.

"It'll be a whole year next month, wont it, darlin'?"

Kevin looked at his wife adoringly and I felt an odd stab of jealousy. Maybe it was because Justin had never shown a shred of inclination that he ever loved me, let alone that he would ever propose. I choked back the remains of my heartbreak, refusing to let it show. I had other things on my mind right now, anyway.

Alana looked at me suddenly, her gaze fixed on my face as if she had just noticed me standing there the whole time.

"You have really pretty eyes, Suzanna. You obviously get those from your mother!" When she smiled, it was so pretty that I had no doubt of why Kevin had fallen in love with her. "And your blonde curls are so cute! She's like a little doll, isn't she, hon?"

I laughed through my closed mouth, refusing to let my disdain for Alana Brady show. She seemed nice enough, and yet I had heard her condescending tone far too many times that day. The kind of tone that suggested I needed to be reassured and molly-coddled like I was some kind of fragile china doll that could break at any second.

Kevin seemed to sense my discomfort as he gave me a wry smile, his kind eyes showing me that our conversation was now over.

"Let's get you home, shall we, darlin'?" I watched as Kevin placed a large hand on his wife's swollen belly. "I'll run you a warm bath, if you like?"

Alana turned to look at me, quite unexpectedly, and I was sure that I detected a hint of spite in her pretty brown eyes. "He's a keeper, isn't he?"

I chuckled at the loved-up couple as Alana took her husband by the hand and led him back down through the hallway.

Just when I thought that was the last time I would see Kevin Brady, I heard a voice echoing back down towards me. "Take care, Suze…"

I looked up to see Kevin grinning at me before he disappeared between a crowd of dark suits and sombre faces.

Chapter 2

I arrived at Dublin Airport at 4:30pm, ready for my 6:30pm flight into Newquay.

I sent a quick text to Fran telling her I would be arriving around 7:45pm so that she could be ready to pick me up.

"You sure you have everything, sweetheart?"

"I'm sure you'll remind me if I don't…" I said, my gaze concentrated on my iPhone. When I looked up, my mother was looking at me sympathetically, as if she was just another one of the mourners back at the house. As if I was the only one in mourning for my father.

"I miss you, Suzanna", she said. I always thought it strange that she called me by my full name, whereas everyone else I knew preferred Suzy, or Suze, (Kevin, namely). I preferred my nickname, to be honest. "You know, if you and Fran are struggling down there to make ends meet, you know you're more than welcome to…"

"We're managing fine, Mum." I spoke bluntly, irritated that my mother was, once again, trying to steal away my independence. It was one of the only things that I held on to these days. What with my recent break-up, and now the loss of my father, my work was all I had.

"Alright, then." I could see my mother wringing her hands in front of her, her delicate gold bangles on her wrists jingling noisily as she debated whether to hug me. In that instant, I noticed how thin she had gotten in the last couple of years. "Well, have a safe flight, sweetheart."

Kissing me politely on the cheek, I smelt the unmistakable scent of Gucci on her collar and I held my breath until she got back into the car.

Just as I turned to make my way through the airport doors, I heard a car door open suddenly. "Suzy?"

I turned to see Graham Connors step out of the driver's seat and make his way over to me. He was tall, just over 6" with a shaved head and kind eyes that I couldn't help but warm to. Even if he was one of my mother's many conquests.

I leant against the metal handle of my little suitcase, waiting for, what I assumed, would be more words of sympathy.

"Don't be too hard on your mother, will you?" His kind, brown eyes were full of concern. "She's been through more than you know."

"What do you mean?" I frowned at him, his words throwing me into a cloud of confusion. "We're both grieving for the same man, Graham. What makes you think she's the only one suffering?"

I heard the malice in my own voice and I saw a flash of hurt appear in Graham's eyes. "I know, Suzy, I know."

"Well, then, try and understand it from my point of view, will you? I've just lost the only person I ever used to look up to!"

Graham stared at me, clearly at a loss for words. "I'm…" Fleetingly, I felt a pang of guilt lodge itself below my bosom. He was trying to comfort me in the only way a step-father knew how. "Of course, I'm sorry." He put his arms around me and I let him for a few seconds before I pulled away self-consciously. "Have a safe flight, Suzy."

"Thank you. Bye."

I smiled thinly, turning on my heel and walking through the double doors towards the check-in area.

When I turned back, Graham was gone and the Audi R8 had already sped away, back to Foxrock and their big house in the country.

I arrived at Newquay airport at 7:50pm and spotted Fran waiting for me in Arrivals.

"Suzy!"

She ran up to me, arms extended outwards, and I had never been happier to see anyone.

Francesca Rice was the ultimate girl-next-door. Her long auburn waves fell just below her delicate bosom and she had freckled skin that made her appear much younger than her twenty-seven years. Her eyes, a warm hazel colour, complimented her tousled waves of hair and I breathed in the sweet scent of coconut that she always seemed to carry with her.

"How are you doing, Baby Blue?"

I smiled at the use of her pet name for me – a name my father always used to call me – and we walked together towards the rear of the airport and out to the car park.

"Not great, given the circumstances, Fran..."

"Ah, babe, I understand." She put an arm around my shoulder as I trundled my suitcase over to her little Ford Fiesta. "It must be so hard. I never knew my father so I suppose it makes it a little easier for me, in an odd sort of way..."

She opened the boot of her car and lifted my case inside. "Listen", she said, reaching up to close the boot. As she did, I noticed her abs looked even more defined since the last time I had seen her. Her skimpy purple crop top highlighted her toned torso perfectly and her black Lycra jogging shorts hugged her rear enviably. "I have big plans for us tonight!"

"Fran, I really don't feel like..."

"Just hear me out!"

I sighed, leaning my palm against the car, knowing it was almost impossible to change Fran's mind when it was already made up.

"I'm taking us home and I'm going to make us both a delicious meal, which will then swiftly be followed by an entire night of binge-eating and the full box-set of Entourage! What do you say?"

She grinned like an excited child and I couldn't help but grin back at her infectious personality. "I'd say that sounds perfect!"

"Yes!" Fran squealed delightedly and hugged me again. "That's my girl!"

We giggled like two naughty school-children as we got in the car, and I felt a sudden rush of relief to be back home to everything that felt safe and familiar.

As we left behind the busy roads and took a left into Mousehole, I rolled down the car window, desperate to smell the sea.

I inhaled deeply, smiling to myself as my life came flooding back to me. I had never been more desperate to return to my work.

I heard Fran chuckling next to me. "You're home, babe!"

"I know!" I sighed, blissfully. "I can't believe how good it feels!"

"Just you wait until we get home!" She glanced sideways at me, and I narrowed my eyes at her.

"What have you done this time?"

"Nothing that you won't be thanking me for, alright!" She giggled mischievously. "Just have a little faith in me, for once!"

I laughed quietly to myself as Fran drove the rest of the way home, wondering what surprises my best friend had left for me this time.

As Fran parked up on the side of the road, I stepped out onto the pavement and was greeted by the welcoming warmth of Cornwall, despite the lateness of the day. It was beautiful for September and I walked over to the wooden fence that looked out over the sea. Leaning my elbows against it, I stared out.

To my left, I could see St Michael's Mount rising from the sea like a great sea creature. It was breath-taking, observing it from this distance and I remembered why I had fallen in love with Cornwall all those years ago. I couldn't wait for daybreak to see the Cornish coast in all its glory.

"So I'll bring everything in myself, shall I?" Fran shouted over at me from the opposite side of the road. She was carrying my little suitcase along with her own sports bag she took everywhere with her and I ran over to her, chuckling to myself.

"Sorry, hon!" I took the suitcase from her and we walked the few metres to our little apartment, tucked away down a neat little alleyway over-looking the harbour. "What's this surprise you've got for me, then?"

"Ha!" Fran cackled as we turned down the narrow alleyway, the wheels of my suitcase wobbling against the uneven cobbles. "As if I'd tell you that!"

Turning the key in the lock, Fran opened wide the white-washed door. My bedroom was situated on the ground floor, so I walked straight into my room, which, in turn, is when I saw it.

"Fran!" I threw my hands to my mouth in shock, staring up at the wall where the head of my bed sat. Tears sprang to my eyes as I took in the size of the canvas. The painting was the entire width of my bed. "How did you…"

"I remember you saying how much you loved it when we went to that gallery in Falmouth." I looked over at Fran, continually amazed at my best friend's generosity. "I put down a deposit for it a few days before you left for Dublin and I paid the rest just yesterday."

I stared at her, incredulous. "How did you afford it? I thought you said you were struggling with the website…?"

Fran shook her head defiantly, a smile spreading across her pretty face. "Not since we've had a sudden influx of customers in the past week or so! Josh got in touch with an award-winning marketing company to give us a hand, you know, with getting our product out to the public and all that." Fran's pretty face was a picture of pride and sheer satisfaction. "We've had emails left, right and centre asking for orders!"

"Fran, that's amazing! I'm so proud of you!" I hugged her tightly and she squeezed me back. "Really, though, this gift is beyond generous of you!"

I clambered onto my bed, shuffling forward on my knees to take a closer look.

A deserted beach with an evening sky of a thousand different colours. That's what had attracted me to it when I had first laid eyes on it just a few weeks ago. 'The End of the Day', it was called.

"Right!" Fran threw my suitcase down onto my bed. "That's enough emotion for one day! Let's crack open a bottle of bubbly, shall we?"

I lounged on our worn old sofa in our modest little apartment, my legs tucked to one side the way I used to do when I was little.

"Was it as hard as you thought it would be, then?"

I looked at Fran, concern filling her big, hazel eyes.

"Harder", I said, staring into my empty wine glass. "You know me, Fran. I don't get emotional, I don't cry…" Fran smiled knowingly at me and I laughed. "Unless my best friend buys me an amazing painting, of course!"

"Thank you!" She raised her glass proudly, already looking a little tipsy.

"Seriously, though", I continued. "The whole four days drained me emotionally. I didn't think I'd make it home in one piece!"

"Good job Miss Rice was here to save you, then, eh?" Fran stood up, a little unsteadily, and made her way over to the open-plan kitchen area. "You want another, babe?"

"Of course!" I tilted my head back, a little too hard, and almost gave myself whiplash. "Give it to me!"

I listened to the glug-glug of red wine filling my glass as Fran poured and heard the distant sound of the sea clashing against the rocks outside our window. It immediately settled me.

"So", she said, sitting back down on the sofa, her glass of wine cradled between three fingers. "You meet anyone?"

I stared at her, knowing Fran's array of expressions all too well and sniggering at her thinly veiled question. "What could you possibly mean by that, Francesca Rice?"

"You know full well what I mean, Suzanna Sharp!" She clinked her glass against mine, so hard that a fracture line appeared in both our glasses. We laughed out loud. "Were there any hotties to distract you?" I smiled to myself, almost absentmindedly, but Fran immediately noticed. "There was?! Tell all!"

She scooted forwards on the sofa excitedly and I found myself blushing, although I didn't know why. "You remember me telling you about Kevin Brady?"

Fran looked to one side, as if thinking, and then realisation dawned on her like a lightbulb being switched on.

"That guy you used to babysit?! Wasn't he like, fifteen?"

"Seventeen!" I laughed, taking another sip of my wine. "But it doesn't matter, anyway. He's married with a pregnant wife now! I could barely believe it when he told me!"

Fran sighed, frustrated, and her concern for my hapless love life warmed my heart.

"Typical! Was she at least as pretty as you?" I smiled, thinking about the way Kevin had placed his hand on his wife's swollen belly affectionately, his love for her evident in his eyes and I felt a sharp pain in my side. "Suzy?"

I must have looked downcast because I felt Fran's hand on my knee, her friendly touch as comforting as a warm blanket on a cold night.

"Sorry, my mind wandered…"

Fran looked at me, wiggling her eyebrows at me mischievously. "You naughty girl!" She downed the last few drops of red wine and placed it determinedly down onto our little coffee table. "Actually, I've been meaning to tell you something…" She cleared her throat, and I could tell she was about to give me some news I didn't really want to hear. "Justin called the other day, left a message for you."

I froze, my grip on my glass tightening. "What did he say?"

Fran's expression turned serious all of a sudden, an expression she very rarely showed in front of me.

"That he misses you." She looked at me carefully, as if trying to gauge my response. "That he'd like to meet up and talk about…things."

I took a deep breath, trying to figure out how I felt about Justin Wright. But my emotions had been through enough in the past few days and I forced the thought away.

"That's something I don't need to think about right now, Fran."

"I did tell him you were away for the funeral", she added, quickly, as if to defend herself. "He had no idea."

"And rightly so!" I scoffed. "I wouldn't have wanted him feeling any sorrier for me…"

Fran nodded, slowly, understandingly, and we sat in silence for a few minutes.

"Well, babe", she said, rising from the sofa with a heavy sigh, "I better hit the sack! Josh and I are meeting with a client tomorrow and I need to be looking fresh and sharp if we want it to go well!" She leaned down to kiss the crown of my head. "Love you, Suzy."

"Love you, too."

Just when I thought I was going to hear her footsteps leading up to our little balcony, Fran crouched on her haunches in front of me.

"You're going to be alright, babe." She smiled warmly at me, and for the first time that day, my confidence lifted, if only a little. "You're a fighter, you know! You always have been."

I smiled back at her, reaching forward to kiss her forehead. "Thanks, Fran. You're the best." I listened to her footsteps ascending the little staircase up to the loft-cum-balcony. "Sleep tight!"

I woke up late, the sunlight streaming through a gap in my curtains and hurting my eyes. Squinting against it, I sat up in bed.

I could tell that Fran had already left as her coat was missing from the rack near the door. Yawning loudly, I made my way upstairs in my pyjamas, the cool, pine-wood stairs creaking beneath my bare feet. It felt good to be home.

I poured fresh water into the kettle and sat down on the sofa, listening to the rising crescendo of the kettle's deafening whistle.

While it boiled, I checked my emails on my iPhone.

I had twelve new emails and thirty three that were spam, clogging up my inbox. I sorted through them, one by one, until I got to two that caught my eye.

The first was from the Cornish Seal Sanctuary asking when I would be back to work. I emailed them straight away saying that I was planning to pop in later that day for an update on the pups' welfare.

The second email was from my mother and I jolted at the subject field. It simply read: *Ring me ASAP xx*

I chewed my thumbnail, debating whether or not to take it seriously. My mother could be a little melodramatic at the best of times. She was probably just ringing to see if I was home safe, which would be odd, I thought, seeing as she's never done that in the past.

Finally deciding to call her, I tapped her number into my phone and waited patiently for the dial tone.

It rang four times before she picked up.

"Sweetheart, is that you?"

"Of course it's me, Mum", I said, sarcastically. "Whose phone do you think this is?"

"Suzanna", she said, ignoring my tone completely, and the edge in her voice alerted me to something more urgent. I sat up slightly on the sofa. "There's been some new information that's surfaced regarding your father's death." My blood ran cold and I could find no words to counter what my mother had just told me.
"Suzanna?"

"Yes..." My voice came out as a broken whisper and I cleared my throat meaningfully. "Yes, I heard you. What... What do you mean, new information?"

I heard my mother exhale heavily from the other end of the line and the phone trembled in my hand.

"The autopsy came back yesterday. They say that your father's heart failure was due to chemicals in his system, and that..."

My throat felt dry. "And what?"

"...And that..." Suzy heard her mother draw in a shuddering breath, "he died of an overdose. Suzanna, I think your father took his own life."

I sat, numb, on the sofa in our living room, the peach-coloured upholstery suddenly making me want to vomit all over it.

"That can't be true, Mum." I shook my head, knowing that she couldn't see me, but also reassuring myself that it had to be a false autopsy. "You must know that's not true, surely?"

"Oh, sweetheart", her cries were louder now, and I couldn't help but feel a sharp pang of guilt for leaving her the way I did. "I don't know what to believe anymore!"

I swallowed back my shock at the unexpected news, trying to be strong for my mother.

"Do you want me to fly back? I can be on the first flight..."

"No, no, of course not!" I heard my mother clear her throat loudly on the other end and the sound of a man's voice, soothing, in the background. "You've only just got back. In fact..." I could almost hear the cogs turning in her mind as I heard her breathing deeply. "I'll fly out to see you first thing tomorrow."

Her words shocked me into speechlessness. It was only when I heard the man's voice again that I managed to force a jumble of sounds from my mouth.

"Mu-Wh-What? You don't have to..."

In the past two years, my mother had never come to Cornwall to visit me. It had never really bothered me as me and my mother had never been close. So it baffled me as to why she would want to do this.

"No, Suzanna. Let me do this. Please." Her voice was firm, and I didn't have the heart to argue with her. I had never heard her sound like that before. It unnerved me. "We need to talk about this together."

I opened my mouth to speak and closed it again, unsure of what to say. I supposed what she was asking made sense, and yet there was an urgency in her words that left me curious as to what her intentions really were.

"Sure", I said, unable to think of anything else to say. "Let me know when you land and I'll pick you up. We're about an hour away from Newquay airport."

"Thank you, sweetheart." Her voice sounded calmer now, and I was amazed at her resilience. Earlier, she had sounded close to a breakdown. Now, she was calm and collected, as if she was someone else entirely. "I'll see you tomorrow, then? I'll text you later tonight with my flight details."

"Alright, no problem." I spoke as if on auto-pilot, still in shock as to what was to unfold tomorrow morning. "Bye, Mum."

"Bye, sweetheart."

She hung up the phone and I stared at the image on my home screen, – a happy, smiling seal pup with big, black eyes beaming back at me – wondering what on earth my mother and I would even need to talk about.

The next day, I deliberately woke up an hour earlier than I had planned to. I needed to prepare my mind for what followed.

I had sent a quick work email, apologising that I wouldn't be in until Tuesday the following week due to unforeseen circumstances. It was the truth, after all.

"So, how long is she staying?" Fran pressed her teabag against the side of her mug with the back of her spoon. "You know we've only got two bedrooms', right?"

I laughed at Fran's outspokenness, silently thankful that my mother had already booked herself a night in a hotel in main town Penzance.

"Just one night. In a little hotel down the road." I chuckled again. "Don't worry, she won't take up any space, if that's what you're worried about!"

Fran stuck her tongue out at me and sat down next to me on the sofa.

"So, what do you think you'll talk about?"

"I haven't a clue." I listened to Fran slurp her tea noisily as I thought about her question. "I suppose she'll ask me if I could think of any reason why my Dad would..." My voice quivered at the thought and I felt Fran's gentle touch on my arm. "It can't be true", I said, again, more to myself than Fran. I leant back against the comfortable old sofa, and closed my eyes. "It just can't."

"It's not like she spent much time with him, anyway."

I could hear the contempt in Fran's voice. She had never warmed to my mother. She had only ever visited her once, with me, for my mother's tenth wedding anniversary a year ago. "You probably knew him a lot better than she ever did."

I let out a heavy sigh, wondering if what Fran said was true.

Chapter 3

I scraped my hair into a high ponytail, my curly blonde rat's tails escaping either side of my temples so that I looked like I had wings.

Untameable. That was me. Maybe that had been why Justin hadn't been able to handle me very well. Maybe he had preferred someone he could settle down with, someone he could start a family with. Everything that I just wasn't ready for.

"Stop it, Suzy." I chided myself, reaching for my make-up bag on my bedside table. "You don't need him."

I very rarely wore make-up – my laziness attributing to that fact – but my porcelain skin looked whiter than white today, so I thought a quick slick of foundation wouldn't hurt.

When I had done, I looked myself over in the mirror next to my bed. The foundation had given me a nice, soft glow and I smiled, pleased with the result. I decided, then, to do the full works. I had started now, I thought, why not finish?

I reached in my little black make-up bag for my black kohl eyeliner and mascara, applying them both liberally to my eyes. When I had finished, I leaned closer to the mirror, widening my eyes to see the effect.

My eyes seemed to pop in a way that actually made me feel quite proud. Their baby blue colour shone, even in the dim light of my room, and it made me think of my mother. She would be here in just a few hours' time, and I still had not the faintest idea what we would both end up talking about. Would she have more information on Dad's death, maybe? Was there something she wasn't telling me?

I told myself I wasn't going to think about the answers to those questions until the time came, and so I hunted in my drawers for some clothes to wear.

Pulling on my navy combats, I rummaged around for my black-and-white striped tee-shirt, choosing instead my red and white one. Stripes were my thing. My wardrobe was basically a treasure trove of nautical-themed clothes. Fran had regularly urged me to have a look at the website – *75% discount,* she assured me – as my wardrobe had not been updated since about 2005. I didn't care. She was the fashionable, athletic one, not me.

Slipping on my comfortable, blue converse trainers, I went to open the front door. Stepping outside, I could see the sky was clear, and yet, there was a cold bite in the air. Stepping back inside to grab my grey hoodie from the rack, I threw it on and started the familiar walk down to the coastline.

I lifted my head skyward, relishing the sensation of the wind against my face as I walked along the coastal path. With the sea to my right, I carried on walking until I reached an impasse. I looked up at the rocks before me, the child inside me getting excitable as I began to climb.

Climbing as high as I could, I chose a smooth, flat rock where I sat down, legs crossed, looking out to sea.

I could smell the salt just a few metres below me and I thought about my father. The first time I had ever visited Cornwall was with my mother and father in 1991.

It had been warmer than it was now but I remember it like it was just yesterday. My father and I were walking, hand in hand, down the promenade in Penzance. I felt safe whenever my hand was in his, like nothing could ever harm me while he was next to me.

"You want another ice-cream, Baby Blue?"

"Yes! Yes!" I jumped up and down excitedly. "Pretty please, Daddy!"

He laughed; a light-hearted chuckle that I still remember to this day because it reminded me of the big orange bear in The Bear in the Big, Blue House – a kid's show I used to watch constantly in the 90's.

"Daniel, she's already had one." I heard my mother somewhere behind us. "It's not good for her teeth."

"Ah, nonsense!" Dad waved his hand dismissively. "My little girl can have another ice cream if she wants, can't she?"

And then he picked me up in his arms, strong and bulky, and I squealed in delight as he spun me around until the promenade became one long blur before my eyes.

My memory was soon interrupted by a vibration in my left trouser pocket. I retrieved my phone and read the message on my phone screen - *Just boarded plane. See you soon, sweetheart xx*

I let out a heavy sigh, steeling myself for my mother's arrival and made my way back along the coastal path and up towards the car park.

I waited in Arrivals for my mother, feeling like Fran had just a few days before, waiting for me.

Except, this time, I wasn't exactly thrilled about seeing my mother again. I didn't know what she had planned, or what she thought she was going to say to me, for that matter. The only thing I knew my mother was good at was her job. Maybe that was the only thing we had in common.

From the crowd of faces that suddenly started to appear through the glass doors, my mother's was the one I spotted first.

She was dressed, of course, immaculately.

Her hair was poker-straight instead of its usual voluminous style and it looked like it had been highlighted again. Ash blonde and caramel, I guessed. Not like I was an expert, I had never let a hairdresser get anywhere close to colouring my hair.

I was reasonably glad to see that she had dressed appropriately, considering she was now in a coastal area rather than her own rural suburb.

Her dark, denim jeans hugged her figure nicely and she was wearing a simple lilac tee-shirt cut to just above her generous C-cup cleavage. That, I only partially envied her for.

"You look good, Mum", I said, trying to keep the conversation light given the events of the past few days. "New hair?"

"You noticed!" Mum laughed dryly as we walked back to the car park together. "I had to swish my new tresses in Graham's face a few times before he even blinked an eye!"

I laughed. Justin was the same whenever I had gone for a haircut. "That's men for you!"

I drove the hour back to Mousehole with my Mum in the passenger seat, who was trying her best to keep the mood light.

"Work alright?"

"I don't go back until Tuesday." I turned the radio down a fraction. "How's your practice doing?"

"Busy", she said, simply, as she looked out the car window. "I'm having to draft legal documents left, right and centre at the moment. Didn't get home until 10:00pm the other night!"

My eyes widened. "Many new clients, then?"

"Tell me about it..." She carried on staring out of the window and when I looked over at her, briefly, I could see something behind her eyes. Stress? Grief? I couldn't tell. "But let's not talk about work, anymore, sweetheart."

She turned back to me, grinning uncharacteristically, and I smiled thinly.

"So", I said, swiftly changing the subject, "what did you want to do today?"

I heard my mother breathe deeply next to me. "How about a walk?"

I parked in the little car park overlooking Mousehole harbour and I noticed my mother's bright blue eyes widen like little jewels when she stepped out the car.

"Oh, Suzanna, this place is beautiful!"

I watched her as she leant over the wooden fence that looked out to sea, her face an odd mixture of pride and sadness.

"I did tell you..." I said, referring to the many times that my mother could have visited me in the last couple of years that I had lived here. "Do you like it?"

"Suzanna..." When she turned around to face me, I was surprised to see tears glistening in her eyes. It left an odd feeling deep in my heart. "I'm so proud of you, sweetheart."

She came over to embrace me, and I didn't quite know what to do with my arms. It was so out of character that I just stood there, letting her hold me like I was a lifeless mannequin.

"Shall we, um, take a walk along the path, then?" I gestured towards the steps that led down to the short coastal walk I had taken earlier.

"Yes", she said, grinning again and I couldn't help but smile at my mother's sudden change of mood. "Let's go!"

When we reached the impasse, I clambered up onto the rocks as I had before.

"Are you sure this is safe, Suzanna?"

"Of course I'm sure!" I looked down at my mother, laughing at her expression as she searched for a place to wedge her brown, leather boot between to hoist herself up onto the rocks. Of course, she wouldn't be seen dead in trainers. "I come here nearly every day!"

"I don't think I can do this, Su..."

"Here!" I offered my hand to her and she tentatively took it. "Wedge your foot in there! It's easy enough!"

I watched her, giggling to myself as my well-to-do mother splayed her legs apart, trying to balance herself against the rocks.

"It's alright, you laughing!" She stood next to me on the rocks, her expression serious. "You're still young and full of energy!"

"Mum, it's not like you're ancient!" I laughed out loud, sitting down on my favourite rock. "How old are you, again?"

"None of your business, young lady!"

We laughed as she sat down next to me. As we listened to the crashing of the sea below us, I felt a sense of euphoria wash over me. A euphoria tinged with sorrow that my father wasn't here with us.
He had always had a deep passion for the sea, just like me.

"Dad would have loved it here."

I didn't realise I had spoken aloud until my mother sniffed loudly.

"You're right. He would have."

We were silent for a long while and I wondered what was going through my mother's mind, all of a sudden.

"Suzanna? The day before your father..." her voice trailed off and I looked across at her, picking at a broken thumbnail. "The day before your father passed, he left me a message on my phone."

I froze against the rock, suddenly feeling the chill in the air stronger now.

"What did he say?"

I saw my mother swallow hard and she winced with the effort, as if she was swallowing glass.

"He apologised to me..." She was visibly shaking now, and despite my initial discomfort, I reached forward and took her hand in mine. "And then he said... that even though you and I had never seen eye to eye on a lot of things, that, deep down, you do love me." My mother turned to me then and I saw tears streaming down her face, smudging her perfectly applied mascara. "Is that true, sweetheart?"

I stared at her, gobsmacked that she would even ask the question.

"Of course I do, Mum!" Tears sprang to my own eyes, more out of amazement that that was the last thing on my father's mind before he died. "You're my mother, aren't you?"

I smiled at her reassuringly, and when she looked across at me, I saw that look behind her eyes again that I couldn't quite read.

"That's just it, sweetheart", she said, slowly releasing her hand from mine. "I'm not..."

Chapter 4

Helen, Ireland, 1988

    I was just twenty-one years old when I met Daniel Sharp.
    If I had known then what I know now, I certainly would not have walked into Cobblestones' that night. I would have carried on down the street, arm-in-arm with my best friend, Sally Lake, and walked into any other bar or pub along King Street.
    But that's not what I did.
    "Another? My round!"
    Bleary-eyed, I turned to Sally, who was already signalling to the bartender for another round of Tequila shots.

"Sally! I've had two already!" From the corner of my spinning eyes, I could see the bartender already pouring two more shots of Tequila. "You know I'm a lightweight!"

I plonked my head, as heavy as a rock, onto the sticky wooden surface of the bar, immediately regretting my decisions that night. I had finals in just two days' time and I was supposed to be using my night to study and cram and whatever else students were supposed to do before a big exam. And yet, here I was, drinking myself under the table on a Saturday night and possibly draining away any chance of me getting a decent job in my chosen field of Law.

"Come on, spoil-sport!" Sally nudged my arm playfully and I nearly toppled from the rickety old bar stool. "Live a little! Besides, we all know you're a Grade A student!"

I looked over at her, her bob of mousy brown hair bouncing against her cheeks. It always bothered me that she never seemed to wear a shred of make-up. She had such pretty features, her clear green eyes large and insightful with razor-sharp cheekbones. But Sally was confident in herself. I had always admired that about her.

"Here!" She slid the shot of Tequila towards me forcefully, a mischievous glint in her pretty eyes. "One more for the road, eh?"

I didn't want to come across as frigid in front of a free spirit like Sally so I downed the shot, slamming it back down onto the hard wooden surface with more force than was necessary. Immediately, I regretted it.

"Is she alright?"

The rich lilt of the bartender's southern accent was lost on me as I heard Sally giggling next to me.

"She's fine!" She spoke between laughter and a part of me wanted to slap her for getting me this drunk when she knew full well that, in just a few days' time, my future was in my hands. "Aren't you, Hel?"

Something gurgled unpleasantly in the very pit of my stomach, and I let out a moan. "I need to be…"

I sprang off the stool as fast as I could, my head lowered to the ground as I pushed past a crowd of people blocking my way to the door.

"Excuse me, I…"

Almost as soon as my feet made contact with the concrete, I doubled over the sidewalk and released the contents of that evening onto the pavement. My throat stung and my eyes watered with the effort.

"Party hard, love?"

I saw two pairs of men's shoes as they walked past me, laughing aloud at my humiliation. I took three deep breaths, running my fingers through my hair and recoiling in disgust as I felt a spool of vomit entangled in the knots.

When, eventually, I stood up, I leant back against the white stone wall of Cobblestones' pub and tried to restore a little bit of dignity.

Taking in my surroundings, I slowly turned my head to one side. It was then that I noticed one other man standing to the other side of me, with only the entrance door of Cobblestones' separating us.

He hadn't noticed me but I couldn't help but stare at him. He was extremely handsome, and yet, I could tell there was something very ordinary about him. The way he stood, his hands shoved into his jean pockets, his white linen shirt half-tucked into them as if he had forgotten to look in the mirror before he had left the house. His hair, a similar mousy-brown to Sally's, was cut short against his head, highlighting finely chiselled features and a speckling of stubble across his square jaw. Much too old for me, I thought, disappointedly.

Just when I thought my observations had gone unnoticed, the man turned suddenly to face me and his gaze nearly brought me to my knees. There was an intensity in his eyes that unnerved me, and yet I found myself curiously drawn to him.

He was staring at me now, almost in the way a predator might stare at its prey and I didn't know whether to run back in to Sally and grab my jacket or wait, curiously, to see what the man would say. The latter held me back, of course.

"Are you alright?"

He had a deep voice and it set my heart to racing. He walked over to me so that he was now stood directly in front of me and out of habit, I lowered my gaze so that I was staring at the buttons on his shirt.

"Yes, thank you, I'm..."

"Hey..." All of a sudden, I felt the rough texture of his forefinger underneath my chin and he lifted it gently so that I had no choice but to look at him. "You're not here alone, are you?"

He was staring into my eyes so forcefully that I could practically feel my heart against my chest. His eyes looked large under the light of the streetlamp next to us, and yet it was too dark to tell the exact colour.

"Um..." I heard my voice tremble slightly and I cursed under my breath for giving me away. "No, I'm here with my friend..."

Almost as soon as I spoke, the door swung open. It would have hit me squarely in the side of the face had the man not pushed me to one side quick enough to avoid it.

"Helen!" Sally came bustling out of the pub, my grey, leather jacket slung over her arm. Her smile was wide, her eyes bright, and a selfish part of me hoped that the man in front of me hadn't noticed her obvious beauty. But when I looked over at him, he was still staring at me intently. My heart raced again. "You certainly look better!" Sally winked at me knowingly and I glared at her. "Shall we get going, then?"

"Yep!" I tried to act as casual as possible as I turned to thank the man in front of me. "Thank you, um..."

"Daniel." He smiled thinly, his gaze still fixed on my eyes. "Daniel Sharp."

"Thank you, Daniel." I bit my lip teasingly – my poor attempt at flirting – and noticed his smile stretch wider, revealing perfectly aligned teeth. "Hopefully see you again?"

He nodded slowly, his gaze now traveling down the length of my body as if assessing me for some kind of project. Oddly, it turned me on.

"I certainly hope so, Helen."

I smiled shyly as I walked a little further down the street, following Sally into the back of the taxi that was waiting for us on the corner.

"Who was that?" I watched Sally retrieve her compact from her purse, holding it up to her face and scrunching her hair up between her fingers for extra volume. Not like she needed it. "He was hot!"

"Daniel", I breathed. "His name's Daniel Sharp."

Just before the taxi sped off down the street, I looked out the car window.

Daniel Sharp had not moved from where he stood and was still staring down the street after me.

"What did he look like?"

I frantically searched Cobblestones' pub for Daniel Sharp, eager to see if I was still in his memory from the previous week and he had been visiting every night since to see if he could find me again. Ridiculous, I knew.

"He's tall."

I sat with my elbows leant back against the bar, scanning the sea of faces that took up the whole floor of Cobblestones' pub. There was a pub quiz tonight, and so there was all sorts in. Mainly pensioners, I noticed, with a pang of disappointment. No sign of any mysterious men with curious eyes to be seen...

"Tall, dark and handsome, eh?" Sally laughed, taking a rather uncouth gulp of Guinness. "How cliché!"

I laughed with her, my mood considerably lighter this week. I had finished all my exams and was quietly confident. It was just a waiting game now. And I was happy to wait. I had spent months revising and cramming, exhausting myself to the point of delirium and I was now looking forward to letting myself go. I was ready to have fun again.

"That's him, isn't it?"

I jerked my head to where Sally was pointing, at the opposite end of the bar.

It was Daniel, for sure. My heart plummeted, though, when I noticed a tall, leggy brunette chatting away to him as if she had known him for years.

"It's always the good ones that are taken, eh?"

I barely heard Sally next to me, the painful lurch of my heart distracting me.

I didn't know why I was so upset. I didn't even know the man. He had barely spoken ten words to me! And yet, there had been something about him that had so intrigued me that he had left me wanting more. I pushed the well of disappointment deep inside me and readied myself for a night that I was determined I wouldn't remember anything of the next morning.

"Helen?"

I jolted at the voice, nearly tumbling from the stool as I turned to see Daniel Sharp walking towards me.

I felt Sally nudge my elbow. "Looks like I was wrong..."

I nudged her back, harder, ignoring her completely. "Daniel!"

"I hope you're not stalking me!"

I blushed violently, biting my lip again. Although, this time, it was more out of embarrassment that he had read me perfectly.

"I was about to say the same!"

He laughed and I noticed two deep-set dimples appear either side of his wide smile. My heart fluttered.

"Can I get you another drink?"

"Look at that! A man after your own heart, Hel!"

I sighed irritably at Sally's garish comment, lowering my head to my brown suede boots and feeling my cheeks burn. Sometimes, I really wished there was an off button for her tongue.

"I'm off to a good start then, am I?"

Daniel stared at me then and I noticed for the first time his hazel eyes, flecked with green, and I couldn't believe a man like this would even look twice at me. I felt like the main character in a Jackie Collins novel. It was surreal.

"I like this one!" Sally whispered it in my ear so he wouldn't hear and I suppressed a self-satisfied smile. "I'm off to the little girls' room!"

I watched her walk away, noticing a couple of older men look up from their drinks and ogle her hourglass figure, decked out in black jeans and a red-checked shirt that barely hid her obvious cleavage.

"So, what do you want?" Daniel pulled out the stool next to me and perched on the end, signalling for the bartender. "No more shots, that's for sure, eh?"

I laughed, embarrassed. "Definitely not! I'll have a glass of white. Thanks."

He ordered my drink, along with a glass of Coke for himself as he was driving, and we sat in an oddly comfortable silence for a while. As soon as the drinks came, I decided to speak what had been on my mind since we had first met.

"Just so you know," I began, fingering the stem of my wine glass nervously, "I'm only twenty-one."

Daniel turned to me after taking a long swig of Coke, looking only mildly surprised. "You look a lot older."

"Really?" I stared at him, his chiselled features more defined now I looked at him up close. He had a nice jawline, I noticed, the speckling of stubble setting it off handsomely and he had a strong nose. Almost Roman-like, I thought. "I'm not sure if that's a compliment or not..."

He grinned at me, and my heart fluttered again when I noticed the dimples crease his pale skin.

"Don't worry, it is." To my surprise, he placed his hand atop of my own. It was brief, but the warmth of his touch was enough to stir my senses and leave me feeling flushed. "I think it's the hair. Very mature and formal."

Absentmindedly, I ran my fingers through my Heather Locklear-styled hair that fell just below my shoulders, highlighted with ash, caramel and golden blonde.

"And I don't think I need to mention how beautiful your eyes are..." He was looking at me again, in the same way he had the week before, the intensity of his gaze leaving me, once again, a little unsettled. "You must hear that all the time?"

I curled a tendril of hair behind my ear, trying to hide the blush that was creeping up my cheeks. I was fond of my baby blue eyes, I had to admit. Even Sally had told me once that she envied me for that, and I always thought that she was the beautiful one.

Just then, Sally appeared like a whirlwind by my side.

"So!" She clapped her hands together, looking from me to Daniel in turn. I noticed she had re-applied her bright coral lipstick. "Who wants to challenge me to a game of pool, eh?"

Daniel looked at me as if to offer me the chance but I politely declined.

"Please", I said, gesturing towards the pool table at the end of the bar where I had spotted Daniel. "Go ahead, if you dare!"

"Oi, you!" Sally smacked me playfully on the arm. "I can play fair!"

"And I'm the Queen of England!"

Daniel laughed at us both as he made his way over to the pool table with Sally.

From where I sat, I watched them both take turns, Sally's competitiveness becoming more and more obvious to the inhabitants of Cobblestones' by the minute. Fortunately, we were regulars to this pub so most of them knew us well.

For Daniel, though, this was his first insight into Sally Lake. If he didn't like my best friend, then there was no hope for us ever beginning a successful relationship.

But as I watched, I noticed the two of them laughing and conversing as if they'd known each other for years. A part of me was glad, but then I knew how flirtatious Sally could be and I began to resent her a little. Daniel potted a red-striped ball into a corner pocket and Sally cheered, patting him on the shoulder in a congratulatory way.

"Nice one, Dan!"

Before I could wallow in my failed attempt to pull, Daniel came over to me. He was smiling broadly, and when he stopped directly in front of me, I wondered what was going through his mind. His hazel eyes were large, and I found myself staring longingly up at him.

All of a sudden, he leant down towards me and cupped my cheek in his hand, bringing my lips to his.

"Woo! Go for it!"

"That's it, son!"

Cries of delight sounded throughout the pub, and I heard Sally somewhere among them. The blood pounded in my ears as Daniel Sharp kissed me harder, and I could do nothing but sink into the passion I could taste in his kiss.

"Don't waste any time, do you, Dan?"

Sally's comment made me giggle as soon as Daniel released his lips from mine, and I stared up at him.

"What was that for?"

Daniel shrugged as if what he'd done was as trivial as the weather outside. "I wanted to kiss you." His matter-of-fact tone made my heart race. "Is that so bad?"

I smiled up at Daniel Sharp, thinking how lucky I was to have met him.

Daniel took me to *The Winding Stair* for our first date. A charming restaurant/bookshop in Dublin City Centre – it was perfect. The food was exquisite, the wine even more so.

I suppose the climax of that night should have rang loud warning bells for me. But Daniel was so charming and funny all night. And I was a sucker for a man that could make me laugh.

"You're telling me that you had no idea that he was gay?" I roared laughing, thankful that the white wine had already settled my initial nerves. When Daniel asked me out at Cobblestones' that night, I had mumbled something so incoherent that he had had to repeat the question to me a second time. "Why else would he have invited you to his plush penthouse suite?"

"I don't know!" Daniel laughed. "Maybe he was just being friendly?" He took a sip of his red wine, leaning back in his chair opposite me.

"Daniel, a straight man doesn't go up to another man in the middle of a club and ask him if he wants to go up to his penthouse suite!" I snorted, a little loud, and a few people looked up from their tables. "You know that, right?"

Daniel grinned at me. "I do now."

I leant back in my own chair and turned my head to look out the window. I could see the bridge over the River Liffey clearly from where I sat. Daniel had booked us a perfect table.

"You like it?"

I sighed contentedly. "It couldn't possibly be any better, Daniel."

He grinned at me, and the look in his eyes set my pulse to racing. "What do you say I pay the bill and we get out of here, eh?"

I grinned back at him. "Sure!" I picked up my little Gucci bag from the floor. "I'm just going to pop to the little girl's room first!"

As Daniel turned the car down a street I didn't quite recognise, I turned to him, puzzled. "Where are we?"

"My place", he said, simply, as if it should have been obvious. "Where did you think we were going?"

"Daniel, I..."

"Helen, relax!" Daniel chuckled, parking up outside a semi-detached house in the middle of an unknown street. "I'm not going to take advantage of you! I'm not like that!"

When he turned to me, I could see in his eyes that he meant it, and I felt a surge of affection for him. Daniel Sharp was a true gentleman.

He reached forward and kissed me gently on the cheek, lingering a while so that I could smell the heady intensity of his Paco Rabanne aftershave. "Unless you wanted to come in, of course..." And then I felt his hand rest on my thigh and I jumped, startled by his sudden touch. "Helen?"

"Daniel, listen, I..." I could feel him staring at me and I swallowed hard, knowing that what I was about to say was sure to have him running back to his house and shutting the door behind him. He probably wouldn't contact me ever again. "I have these...principles."

"Principles?" A smile played on his lips. "What do you mean, like, beliefs?"

"Yes, I suppose." I cleared my throat, struggling to meet his unusually intense gaze. "I don't... I don't agree with sex before marriage."

His hazel eyes widened. I knew it. This was the end. I was waiting for his polite goodbye, when...

"That's fine." He grinned, and I stared at him, mouth agape. "Let's take things slow, shall we?"

I couldn't believe what he was suggesting. All my other boyfriends had run a mile when I had voiced my beliefs to them, and now, here I was, sitting opposite a man who could have had any woman he wanted, telling me he was willing to wait for even marriage to bed me!

Just then, the door to Daniel's house opened and a woman stepped out. She was wearing a pale blue uniform and I thought she looked a little like a maid.

What I noticed, though, was that she was holding a sleeping toddler in her arms. "Senor Sharp?"

"Daniel?" I stared at the woman and the child in bewilderment, unable to take my eyes away. It was as if a warning bell had chimed in my head even then. "Whose child is that?"

When Daniel turned back to me, his face had darkened and, for just a moment, I felt frightened. "She's mine."

I practically choked on my disbelief. "What?!"

"Helen, please, I can explain..."

"I think it's pretty self-explanatory!" I opened the car door, knowing full well that I had no idea where I was, so I couldn't exactly

storm off. But I needed to breathe fresh air. This was too much.
"When, exactly, were you planning on telling me this, Daniel?"
"Helen, please, can you get back in the car?"
Daniel rattled off something in Spanish back to the woman waiting at the door, and I saw her close the door behind her with a suspicious look in my direction.
"Please, Helen..." Daniel leant over the passenger seat towards me, his eyes wide as they looked at me pleadingly. I had never seen anyone look as desperate as Daniel Sharp did in that moment. "Let me explain."
Drawing in a shaky breath, I obliged him and sat back down on the passenger seat.
"Go ahead..." I said, bluntly, refusing to meet his eye. I didn't even bother to shut the car door.
"Her name is Suzanna. My daughter, that is." He cleared his throat, as if preparing himself for what was to come. "Her mother's name was Miriam."
I exhaled slowly, my heart feeling like it was going to explode out of my chest. I had been so close to falling for Daniel Sharp that the pain was almost too much to bear. How could he have kept this from me?
"What happened?"
I looked at Daniel from the very corner of my eye, so much so, that I gave myself a headache doing so.
"She died in childbirth. Two years ago now." His words were clipped, sharp, like a knife to my side and I noticed that he was staring at the gearbox with a faraway look in his eyes. I couldn't help but feel sorry for him, and yet...
"I need to know something."
"What?" He looked up at me then and I found myself drawn to the flecks of green in his eyes.
"What is this, you and me?" I tried to hide the tremble from my voice but I was sure Daniel could see the pain reflected back at him. "Am I just part of a grieving process for you? Because if I am..."

"No!" He took me in his arms then, and before I could stop myself, I found myself sobbing against him. I felt like a foolish teenager, falling for a man so much older than me. "Of course not! I'm having so much fun with you, Helen! I feel like we have something really special, don't you?"

He pulled me away from him, staring at me intensely and I felt my heart begin to race again. I let him wipe a tear from my eye, and I nodded, feebly, weakly.

"Tell me you feel the same, Helen." I saw the desperation in his eyes again, so large and urgent that I couldn't help but acquiesce. "Please."

"Of course I feel the same, it's just…"

"What?" He leaned forward to kiss my cheek again and I felt his stubble graze my chin. "What is it?"

"It's just that your life's so complicated now, Daniel!" I noticed his eyes resting on my lips. "What if it gets too complicated between us?"

"Then we don't let it." He gave me a simple smile, one that told me my words had had no effect on his decision. "You have faith in us, don't you, Hel?"

I looked down, still feeling the rough texture of his hand against my cheek. I knew my head and my heart were at war, and I knew that one of them was going to end up winning. I just wish I knew then the consequences of my next few words.

"Of course", I said, finally. I kissed him gently on the mouth, the refreshing tang of peppermint lingering in my mouth. "Why not?"

Daniel Sharp proposed to me after just six weeks together.

It was a whirlwind romance for sure, but Daniel and I had a connection that I had never felt with anyone else.

Suzanna never even became an issue. I went round regularly to see Daniel and Suzanna, and was surprised to feel my maternal instinct kick in, quite unexpectedly, at that. I had never thought that part of me existed, and yet, whenever Daniels little girl looked up at me – her big, blue eyes large and inquisitive – I felt my heart swell with love for her.

Even Sally had seen the change in me.

"I can't believe it!" She squealed excitedly in the middle of my one-bedroom flat. "Show me the ring again!" I laughed, offering my hand to her like a true lady, and her mouth dropped open. "That is stunning, Hel! How much does that guy make, anyway?"

"Not much, really." I shook my head in wonder, admiring my gold band with the tiny white-gold jewel in the centre. "He only works as a lecturer at the University!"

Sally stared at me, green eyes as wide as saucers. "This one is definitely a keeper, Hel!"

"He is, isn't he?" I giggled girlishly, hearing my phone ring from across the room. "One sec, hon!"

I left Sally in the living room while I went to answer my phone. "Hello?"

"Helen!" It was my father. "When were you planning on telling us you were engaged to be married?"

My mouth dropped open. I hadn't even had the chance to tell my parents yet. Daniel had only just proposed to me that day. I couldn't believe he had already told them without letting me know first...

"I...When did he...?"

"Darling, this is far too soon! You're only twenty-one, for goodness' sake!"

I took a deep breath, glancing through the little alcove of my kitchen into my living room. Sally was reading my copy of Vogue.

"Dad, I'm old enough to make my own decisions!" A part of me wanted to punch Daniel for being so reckless. "Besides, I love him!"

I heard a sigh on the other end of the line. "He's eight years older than you, darling! I'm worried about what his intentions really are..."

"What's that supposed to mean?" I asked him, anger bubbling in my stomach. Daniel had only ever been kind and respectful to me and he had never proved otherwise. I trusted him completely.

"You know full well what I mean, Helen", my father said, his tone all too familiar. "Besides, I thought you wanted to concentrate on your career right now? You told me just the other day you got accepted for a paid internship at that firm, Baker & Nesbitt?"

"I know, and I have!"

"Then why not wait a little and see where that goes?"

"Because I love Daniel and I want to marry him!" I punctuated each word forcefully. "What is so wrong with that?"

By the end of the conversation, my voice was hoarse and I noticed Sally look up from her magazine. I was almost on the verge of tears.

Just when I thought my father had hung up the phone, I heard a quiet voice on the other end. "It's your choice, darling…"

"Yes, it is", I said, before he could say anymore.

"Very well." I heard his heavy breathing on the other end. "Don't forget to send your mother and I an invitation, will you?"

And then he did hang up, and I leant against the kitchen countertop, trying to regain my breath.

"Hel, are you alright?" Sally ran into the kitchen and placed an arm around me. "What happened?"

"I can't believe he told them already." I stared at the grainy countertop, stained with tea and coffee.

"Who?"

"Daniel." I looked at her, my body exhausted from my altercation with my father. "I thought he would at least wait for me to tell them…"

I felt Sally's body rise and fall with each breath. "He loves you, Hel", she said, her tone ever-reassuring. "He was probably just excited to let them know."

I leant my head against her shoulder, inhaling her comforting scent of cocoa butter and tried to forget all about it.

"I really wished you would have let me tell them", I said, under my breath, as we waited in line at City Hall to be registered. "My Dad went berserk on the phone last week!"

"I'm sorry, baby", Daniel soothed, sticking his bottom lip out like a mardy child and enclosing me in his comforting embrace. "I was just so happy to call you my fiancé that I wanted to shout it from the rooftops!"

He puffed out his chest and threw his head back, opening his mouth wide and I quickly clamped my hand over it.

"What are you doing?!"

Daniel chuckled just as I noticed two figures walking up to us.

"Darling?" My well-dressed father came striding up to me, his full head of raven hair glistening with richly applied gel. My mother was beside him, looking as radiant as ever, her perfect blonde curls bouncing with each step she made. She leaned in to kiss Daniel on the cheek as my father kissed me tenderly on my own, speaking close to my ear. "You look beautiful."

"I'm happy you're both here", I said, my voice just as quiet.

"Well, I'm not going to miss my only daughter's wedding, am I?"

My father grinned, his familiarly crooked smile calming my nerves a little as the couple at the register desk took their leave. We were now second in line.

Suddenly, I noticed Daniel take my father to one side. As my mother began to ask me trivial things like, what colour to paint the kitchen, the bedroom, the bathroom, and so on, I tried to listen to two conversations at once. It was hard, I have to admit.

"Mr McKenzie, I just want to thank you for being so supportive with all of this. And I want you to know, I love your daughter very much and I'll do everything in my power to take care of her."

"I hope you will, son", I heard my father say.

"And I can assure you, my daughter isn't an issue." I felt my whole body tense at Daniel's words. "I'm sure Helen's already made that clear to you."

"I-I'm sorry?"

"Dad? Can I have a word?" I rushed over to them both, my feet like lightning as I manoeuvred my father to the far corner of the large entrance hall. My heart was pounding in my chest as my father glared at me, his face turning an unsightly shade of maroon. "It's not what you..."

"Are you pregnant?"

"No!" I felt my hands grow clammy, my white, lace M&S dress sticking in places I didn't know existed. "Of course not! It's..."

"Then what is he talking about, Helen?"

I looked into my father's eyes, full of fatherly concern, and a part of me wanted to embrace him and never let go. But I loved Daniel. The thought of losing him was too much for me to bear.

"He has a two-year old daughter. From another marriage. His wife died in childbirth." My voice was shaking, afraid of what my father's reaction would be. "Dad, I know it sounds complicated, but I love him! And I love Suzanna, she's the perfect little..."

"Darling", he said, his handsome brown eyes locking mine meaningfully. I could almost hear the warning bells ringing in my ears, but I silenced them in my mind. "Listen to me carefully. This man is not right for you, there's just too much for you to..."

"Dad, please, don't do this..." I begged him, and my throat hurt painfully, trying to swallow the lump rising in my throat. "I can be happy with Daniel! He loves me!"

"Helen?" Daniel called over to me suddenly. "We're next!"

"Darling!" My father turned my face to his with the crook of his finger. "Do you really want to throw away a promising career at twenty-one so that you can be second best to that man and his child?"

I stared at my father, my chest heaving as I tried to arrange my jumbled thoughts.

"I'm not throwing anything away, Dad." I clenched my jaw with the effort it took to look my father straight in the eye. "I love Daniel and I am marrying him today." I had to force each word from my trembling lips. "Whether you like it or not."

My father stared at me for what seemed like an age before he lowered his gaze to the marbled floor of City Hall.

"Very well." He straightened, pulling the buttons of his jacket together, as if coming to a decision. "Then I have to leave." His voice was cold and calm. "I can't watch you do this, darling…"

A sharp cry of anguish left my lips almost involuntarily, as I watched my father walk out the large oak doors and descend the steep stone steps.

I sat on the edge of Daniel's queen-size bed in my white, lace dress, staring out of the window. The bedroom of his semi-detached house overlooked a lush, green field, where I could see about four, no, five horses grazing peacefully.

"I can't believe he just walked out like that."

I heard Daniel exhale deeply from somewhere behind me. "Neither can I, if I'm honest." He walked around the side of the bed where I sat, crouching in front of me and taking my hand gently in his. He looked so handsome in his navy suit, the material clinging to his athletic build perfectly. "I always thought your father was a decent man."

I stared at Daniel, surprised by his callous use of words. "He is a decent man, Daniel. He's just…"

"Just what?" Daniel's hazel eyes widened on mine. "I think the word you're looking for is over-protective, Hel."

"I was going to say, he was just looking out for me!" I said, probably a little too defiantly. "Like any father would."

"You're defending him now, are you?" Daniel stood up slowly, loosening his tie and placing it down on his chest of drawers opposite the bed. "Great start to the marriage, that. Choosing the father over the husband, already!"

"Daniel, don't be like that!"

"I'm sorry!" He laughed, throwing his hands up in mock surrender, although I didn't find what he said remotely funny. "Look, this is our wedding night, Hel, and we're already arguing!" I felt the bed give with the weight of him as he scooted over to me from behind. "How about I start relaxing these muscles, hmm?"

I let out a long breath of air through my nose as I felt Daniel's hands begin to caress my neck. I felt the knots loosen and my body temperature begin to rise.

His lips were against the side of my neck and a shiver of pleasure rippled up my back, releasing an unexpected moan from my lips.

"You're mine now, Helen Sharp..."

He tilted me back against the bed, nuzzling his head into my neck as I felt his hand cup my waist eagerly.

My back arched in pleasure and I bit my lip, smiling at the thought that I now belonged to Daniel Sharp.

It was wedded bliss for the next two or three weeks for Daniel and I. We made love nearly every night and I could never have predicted how happy married life made me.

The nursery was at the end of the hall and I loved checking in on Suzanna, offering to help Mrs Jimenez whenever I had a free day.

Daniel left for work every morning at 7:00am, but not without leaving me little notes on my pillow, telling me how much he loved me and couldn't wait to be back home to be with me. I hugged each little yellow Post-it to my chest like an excited child and kept them all in a little box under my bed as keepsakes.

I left him little notes around the house, too. Saucy ones, I might add. Just to leave him interested and wanting more. He had been quite distracted lately with work, having to grade about fifty papers by the following week.

I made a decision, then, to surprise him. I asked Mrs Jimenez if she could look after Suzanna for just a night so that Daniel and I could be alone. I didn't think it would be a problem as she only lived a couple of houses down from us and Daniel had done the same so many times before when he left for various business trips. He trusted Marina Jimenez implicitly.

I opened the bottom drawer of my dresser and pulled out my black, lace baby-doll that I had bought just the other day with the money I earned from my internship.

I slipped it on and looked at myself in the mirror. It hugged my bosom nicely, giving them a little bit more lift and the floaty material skimmed the very tops of my thighs. Reaching for my crimson lippie from my make-up bag, I applied some liberally and pressed my lips together a few times. Just as I was running my fingers through my long, tangled tresses, I heard the turning of a key in the lock downstairs.

Smiling to myself, my heart pounding a little in my chest as to what Daniel would think of the look, I tiptoed to the landing. Standing seductively at the top of the stairs, I waited patiently for him to notice me.

"So", I said, when he finished hanging his coat up against the rack, "what do you think?"

Daniel looked up at me, his face the very epitome of exhaustion.

"Helen, what are you doing?" He sighed wearily, not even raising a curious eyebrow at my revealing attire.

"What does it look like, baby?" I bit my lip teasingly. "I'm trying to seduce you!"

"Well, don't", he said, bluntly. "I'm too tired. Besides, you look like a slut. Go and put some clothes on!"

His response winded me, as if someone had just punched me in the stomach. "Daniel, I was just..."

"Miriam! Shut up!"

I froze where I stood, his words disabling me. "What did you call me?"

I watched Daniel press two fingers against his forehead, as if trying to relieve his stress levels. "Forget it. I've just had a long day." He rested his briefcase against the arm of the sofa. "I'll be up in a minute."

I took a deep breath, barely able to believe what I had just heard pass my husband's lips and wondered if he even realised he had just called me by his dead wife's name.

"Helen, where's Suzanna?"

I heard Daniel calling to me from the other end of the hall. I immediately felt myself tense at the tone in his voice. Now fully clothed, I made my way down to the nursery.

I walked in, noticing Daniel stood over Suzanna's cot, hands clenched into fists by his side. "She's at Marina's", I said. "I asked her if she could look after her for one night so that we could…"

"You did what?"

He stared directly at me, his hazel eyes darkening to a point that left my heart pounding. But not in the way it was used to. "Daniel, I just thought…"

"Who do you think you are to be making decisions about my daughter without my permission?"

I stared at him, his words lodging painfully in my heart. "She's my step-daughter, Daniel", I said, as calmly as my voice would allow. "Don't you think I have a right to…?"

"No! I don't!" He shouted, and it was the first time I noticed that Daniel looked scared. It was as equally frightening to me as I had always thought of my husband as confident and self-assured. The man in front of me had morphed into someone entirely different before my eyes. "I want you to ring Marina Jimenez straight away and ask her to bring my daughter around, now!"

I stood for a while in the doorway, still in shock at Daniel's outburst. "I said, now, Helen!"

Unable to look at him directly in the eye, I left the room, my hands shaking slightly by my side and went downstairs to call Marina Jimenez.

As soon as I heard the doorbell, I breathed a sigh of relief.

"Marina!" I took Suzanna from Marina's motherly arms, holding her in the crook of my arm. "Thank you so much! I'm sorry I called in such a state, I was just…" I tried my best to think of a reasonable excuse for Daniel's behaviour. "I was just worried about her, that's all!"

Marina frowned at me and I wasn't sure whether it was because she didn't understand me or whether it was out of concern. "Are you alright, Senora?"

"Yes. Si!" I said, hastily, remembering some of my high school Spanish. "Thank you, Marina! See you tomorrow! *Hasta mañana!*"

She nodded at me, still looking a little concerned and turned back down the path.

Closing the door behind me, I jumped to see Daniel watching me closely from the top of the stairs. "Give me my daughter, Helen."

I ascended the stairs slowly, Suzanna snoring gently against me until I was stood in front of him. I handed her over as carefully as I could without a word.

Before I descended the stairs again, I felt Daniel's hand clamp itself around my wrist.

"Don't ever make any more decisions about my daughter without my permission again. Do you hear me?"

I nodded wordlessly, his eyes boring into mine and sending a cold shiver down my spine.

I waited for him to lay his daughter down in her cot before I felt safe enough to descend the stairs.

"Helen?"

I looked up from my computer to see Daniel standing in the bedroom doorway. I was in the middle of filling out an application for the post of a Legal Secretary and I really didn't feel like engaging him in conversation after the events of earlier.

"Did you want anything to eat?"

I noticed his hazel eyes were wide and bright – the polar opposite of how they had looked just hours earlier.

"No, thank you."

I turned back to my computer without another word, pretending to read the job description. I was determined for Daniel to see how much he had upset me.

"Helen, I'm sorry..." He came over to the little desk in the corner and perched on the edge, folding his arms across his chest. "It's just that this past week has really stressed me out, what with grading papers, and..." I looked at him over my reading glasses. "I know I shouldn't have taken it out on you."

"No", I said, slowly, carefully. "You shouldn't have."

"You're right." He looked down at the navy blue carpet, as if thinking what to say next. "How about I make it up to you?"

He grinned and I found myself grinning back. "How, exactly, would you do that?"

"Oh", he said, taking my hand in his and bringing it slowly to his lips. "I can think of a few ways..."

He picked me up from my chair and threw me, squealing, onto the bed, and I soon forgot the doubts that had begun to surface in my naïve, young mind.

Months passed and I found myself juggling a career and a family, surprised at the thrill that it was giving me.

I blew gently on my steaming mug of tea as I walked into Daniel's office next door to the nursery.

I could hear Suzanna playing with her soft toys - assigning each of them their own animated voices - and I smiled. I couldn't believe how much my love for that little girl grew with each passing day – I loved her like she was my own.

"Babe?" I spoke carefully, knowing that he didn't like being interrupted when he was busy grading papers.

"Hmm?"

"I've just had an email from work." I watched Daniel lay down his pen and look up at me through his glasses. The thick, tortoiseshell frames made him look so handsome that I wanted to rip them off his face and kiss him hard. But I restrained myself. "They're having an office party at the end of the month. Did you want to go with me?"

"Sounds fun! When is it?"

He grinned at me and I walked over to him, happy that he was in a relaxed mood. I sat on his lap and took off his tortoiseshell glasses, placing them carefully back down onto his desk along with my mug of tea. "Saturday 19th." I kissed him softly on the lips, his stubble tickling my lips. "I'll wear something sexy for you, shall I?"

He laughed, kissing me back, harder. "Nothing too sexy! Don't want anyone thinking you're available!"

I giggled like a naughty child and ran downstairs, letting Marina know that we would be away for the night of the 19th October.

Three weeks flew by and I could hardly believe it was almost November.

Daniel and I had almost been married a whole year.

We arrived at the venue at around 7:30pm, and I stepped out of the slick, black limo that Daniel had hired to take me and a few of my colleagues there. I had tried to talk him out of it as I knew how expensive it would have been for him but he insisted, as always. *Only the best for my second favourite girl*, he had said, and my heart had sank a little. My father's words at City Hall had spiralled back to my mind in an instant when he had said that and I forced them away.

I linked my arm through Daniel's, a couple of my colleague's following behind me. Julia and Simone, two girls about my age, scuttled past me in their stilettoes, turning back to me with a wink.

"See you both inside!"

I grinned at them – two young, single girls clearly on the prowl – and I felt lucky to be on the arm of a man like Daniel. He was confident, sexy and knew how to hold a room. That was clear as soon as we walked through the elegant glass doors into the foyer.

Men and women holding champagne flutes stared at us both curiously, although I knew they were staring at Daniel. They knew who I was, after all.

I paraded him around the hall the entire night, showing him off to my colleagues like I'd won the gold at the Olympics.

He chatted to everyone easily, just like I knew he would, and I stood beside him politely. Maybe I was his trophy wife, I thought, with a sly smile.

"You've done well for yourself with this one, haven't you, Daniel?" Graham Connors - one of Baker & Nesbitt's up-and-coming barristers - gestured towards me with a mischievous grin. "One of the finest assets to the team, Helen is!"

"Oh, stop it, you!" I said, patting Graham playfully on the arm. "You'll give me a big head!"

"It's the truth!"

I could have imagined it, but I was sure I felt Daniel's arm stiffen against my own.

"I think I'm going to get myself a drink", Daniel said, suddenly, and I thought it a little rude to change the subject so quickly. "Do you want anything, baby?"

Daniel brought his lips to my cheek and kept them there for at least a couple of seconds. I looked up to see Graham grinning at me mischievously and I felt myself blush. "Yes, please, babe. I'll have a champagne, if you're offering."

"Two champagne's coming up!" He did a double take at Graham, as if forgetting he was there. "Oh, did you want a drink, Greg?"

"It's Graham", he corrected, his manner far more pleasant than I was finding Daniel's at that moment. "And I suppose one more tipple wouldn't hurt!"

"Ah, sorry!" He chuckled, although I knew Daniel's light-hearted chuckle well, and what I heard certainly wasn't genuine. "My mistake!"

I watched him move to the opposite side of the hall, weaving between men and women chatting, flirting and whatever else people did at office parties.

"He's a mysterious one, isn't he?" Graham tipped the contents of his glass down his throat with one gulp. "Where did you find him?"

"In a bar, of all places!" I said, laughing dryly. "Not that mysterious, really." Graham laughed heartily, leaning close to my ear. "The more mystery, the better, I'd say! Keeps things exciting, don't you think?"

Just then, Daniel appeared at my side, holding two champagne flutes.

"Here you go, baby!" He handed one glass to me, turning to Graham and feigning disappointment. "Sorry, mate, I've only got two hands, I'm afraid!"

"'Course you have!" Graham laughed again, and I smiled at him for being such a good sport in front of my mysterious husband. "I'd be worried if you had more!"

I snorted into my drink at Graham's joke and I felt Daniel turn and glare at me from the corner of his eye.

"One more of these, then, baby, and I think we'd better get going." Daniel lifted his glass to me and I heard the edge to his voice. "Don't want to be late for pre-natal classes tomorrow, do we?"

I stared at Daniel, trying to stop my jaw from dropping to the floor.

"Pre-natal?" Graham frowned, his smile dropping briefly. "Isn't that…"

I noticed his gaze oscillate from me to the glass in my hand and I couldn't believe what Daniel had just done.

"Graham, I…"

"Six weeks already!" Daniel placed a hand on my flat belly. "Can you believe it? We're going to be parents!"

"Well!" I looked up at poor Graham, his shocked expression showing me he was at a loss for words. "Congratulations, Helen!"

My mouth was still open in shock and I was just about to speak up when Daniel took me by the hand.

"Let's get you home, shall we, baby?" Daniel's large, hazel eyes fixed on mine. "I'll run you a bath, if you like?"

And then he led me, wordlessly, out of the hall, leaving me breathless with rage and confusion.

"Do you have any idea what you've just done?!"

"What do you mean?"

I watched, my body still frozen over in shock as I watched Daniel calmly remove his shirt and tie.

I stood in the doorway of our bedroom, staring at my husband, dumbfounded. "Daniel!"

"Helen", he sat down on the edge of the bed and looked at me. "I did you a favour, if anything! I was actually expecting a thank you, if I'm totally honest!"

"Oh!" I couldn't hold back an incredulous laugh. "Yes! Of course, Daniel, thank you for almost costing me my job and making one of the leading lawyers of my company think I'm a boozing pregnant mother-to-be!" I walked over to the window, pulling the curtains shut with an angry swipe. "Thanks a bunch!"

When I turned around, I gasped in shock when I bumped straight into him, standing over me like a shadow. When he spoke, his voice was so low, that, if anyone else had been in the room with us, I still would have been the only one to hear his words.

"When are you going to learn that all I'm trying to do is protect what we have?"

I stared up at him, unable to think of a single word to say in reply and feeling my heart pound against my ribcage.

"Daniel, I'm sorry, I didn't mean to..."

"Forget it", he said, bluntly. "I'm too tired."

And then I watched – mouth agape – as he made his way around the bed, climbed onto the silken sheets and switched off his side-light.

Meanwhile, I could hear the cogs in my own mind turning as I fought desperately to figure out how I was going to sort my own little 'problem' out by Monday.

The following week at work, I had had to reluctantly explain to everyone at work, and of course, Graham Connors about my 'pregnancy'.

On the bus ride to the Baker & Nesbitt offices, my mind had raced with possible explanations; a miscarriage, maybe? No, my conscience wouldn't allow myself to make up such a heinous lie. After all, women miscarried all the time, with great cost to their own mental and emotional health.

Eventually, I had decided to put it down to a phantom pregnancy. I had read about them online and it was a perfectly plausible excuse. My co-workers had thought no less of me and I was relieved to know my goal to progress in the company would carry on as normal.

Of course, I had to admit, Daniel's behaviour the previous night had ignited a hot spark of fear inside me and I couldn't help but wonder about our future together.

I sat at my little office cubicle, munching absentmindedly on a cereal bar when I felt a hand on my shoulder.

"Helen, how are you feeling?"

It was Graham. His kind eyes searched mine, as if he was looking for something specific in my expression and his concern warmed my heart.

"I'm fine, really, Graham. Just a little shaken up, of course, but I'll be fine." It was the truth, after all. Daniel's behaviour the previous night had left me more on edge than ever and it was a relief to admit my true feelings to someone else. It was an added bonus that it was to someone as understanding as Graham.

"'Course you will, love." His kind smile lit up deep brown eyes and I suddenly realised how much I treasured Graham as a friend. "Let me know if you need anything, won't you?"

Just then, from the corner of my eye, I noticed the entrance doors of Baker & Nesbitt open and I saw Daniel standing there, a huge bouquet of red roses in one hand.

Graham turned to follow my awed gaze and my heart somersaulted inside of me. I told myself it was out of happy surprise, but I couldn't deny the shiver of fear that slipped down my spine when I noticed Daniel's eyes rest on Graham, still standing to one side of me.

The darkness in Daniel's hazel eyes, though, soon dissipated and I watched, silently as he walked towards me, grinning wildly. I listened to the 'ahh's' and 'how romantic!'s' from the swooning secretaries as he made his way through the maze of cubicles until he reached my own.

"Hello, um, Graham, wasn't it?" Daniel extended out a hand towards Graham, and I noticed the genuine look of warmth in my husbands eyes. "We met at the office party?"

"We certainly did!" Graham shook Daniel's hand, his smile genuine, as always. My gaze oscillated from my husband to Graham, noticing that my co-workers expression of complete bewilderment mirrored my own. I hid a smile. It seemed that my husbands sudden change of character had taken us both by surprise. "Now it seems that I'm intruding on something quite special, so I'll be promptly leaving, I think!"

I nodded a goodbye to Graham and my gaze fell to Daniel's once again. He perched himself on the edge of my pinewood desk, the bouquet of roses still held high in one hand and I felt my face warm as he stroked my cheek with the crook of his finger.

"Just something to let you know how much I love you, baby..." From the corner of my eye, I noticed Teresa Jones - PA to the Managing Director - peeking over her own cubicle to flash me a secret smile and I blushed harder. "And, also, to say I'm sorry, Helen..."

Those beautiful hazel eyes settled on mine and - like the appearance of a rainbow after a storm - I forgot about the arguments, the careless words that sometimes felt like a knife to my side, and I saw instead the strong, self-assured man I had fallen in love with.

"Thank you, Daniel". I took the flowers from his proffered hands and brought them to my nose, inhaling deeply and slowly. The smell filled my soul, as if Daniel's love seemed to emanate from the petals themselves. "It's me who should apologise, though..." I found myself saying. "I over-reacted when I said you'd cost me my job. Daniel, there's a role being advertised internally for a paralegal, and

Graham himself said that there's no reason why I shouldn't apply as I have more than enough experience!"

Daniel smiled deeply into my eyes and I wasn't entirely sure whether he had heard what I had just said.

"Helen", he said, taking my hand in his, and, just like that, my thoughts were no longer on my job prospects, but on the man in front of me - The man I had fallen so desperately in love with nearly a year ago. "I want to take you out tonight. To *The Winding Stair?* Where we had our first date?"

I smiled at the memory. "How could I forget?"

"Then it's settled." And then Daniel reached forward, pulling me up from my office chair and kissing the tip of my nose. "I'll drop Suzanna off at Marina's later and then I'll pick you up straight after work. I'm going to treat you like the lady that you are!"

Oblivious to the surreptitious glances of my co-workers all around us, he kissed me passionately on the mouth.

Whoops of encouragement sounded throughout the office, reminding me of how he had done the very same thing on that special night in Cobblestones'.

I fell into Daniel's arms once again, my screaming doubts from the night before now little more than whispers at the back of my mind.

At 4:51pm, my fingers raced across the keyboard, desperate to finish the minutes I had been typing up for the past hour.

"Helen, get yourself on home to that husband of yours! I'm sure he's ravenous for you!"

Graham Connor's deep voice travelled through the maze of cubicles towards me. There was just myself, Graham, and Teresa left in the office and I could see through the transparent glass doors in front of me, that the evening was already darkening. I groaned inwardly. I hated catching the bus home in the winter months.

As I typed, I chuckled at Graham's brazen remark, remembering my passionate husband's behaviour just a few hours earlier. At least I wouldn't have to walk home alone tonight.

"One more sentence to do, Gray, and... Done!" I tapped the last letter with a satisfied flick of my wrist, clicked Save on my Word Document, and started to pack my things, eager for my date with Daniel.

Work commitments had left us both feeling a little strained in the past few months and I was determined that tonight would be the fresh start that we both needed.

"Teresa, would you lock up for us, sweet'eart?" I heard Graham call out from further down the office. His accent - an amusing mixture of Irish and Cockney London - always made me smile despite myself. "I'll walk out with Helen, if that's alright with you, love?"

"'Course! Daniel should be here any moment, anyway!" I blushed, quite unexpectedly, as if the ring on my finger wasn't enough to explain Daniel's constant presence in my life. As if Daniel was here, lingering in the shadows of the office space, listening to see how his wife of one year portrayed him to her fellow colleagues. I resented him for that, if only slightly.

"We better be quick, then, eh?"

Graham was standing by the door, holding it open with one hand and I threw on my navy-blue Mac in haste. I smiled at his thinly-veiled comment, sure that I could detect the knowing look in my colleague's keen eye.

When he followed me out of the large glass door and into the bitter night, I shivered with the cold. It was much colder than I had anticipated.

"Here, love, take this!" Graham unfolded his tartan scarf from around his neck, placing it around my own scarf-less décolletage. His fingers touched my collarbone and I was sure I saw his olivey skin redden in embarrassment. "You surprise me, Helen", he said, dismissing his own faux-pas. I couldn't help but admire Graham's modesty, in that moment. "We're in the depths of winter and you don't even remember a vital piece of clothing like your scarf!"

"I know", I said, laughing politely. I sensed Graham had had a crush on me for a while, but I had made careful sure that I gave him no signals that I was interested. Besides, I was married. And I loved Daniel.

"Well", I said, decidedly, sucking ice-cold air in between my teeth and trying to lock down the conversation as kindly as I could. I knew what Daniel would think if he saw me now... "I better be heading off. Apparently, I'm being wined and dined, if you hadn't already heard!"

Even in the darkness, I was certain that I glimpsed a flash of regret pass through Graham's kind eyes. But, as ever, he dismissed it like the gentleman he always was.

"Of course, yes!" He patted my arm, as if I was a small child on my way to school and, I had to say - much to my discredit - his discomfort made me smile. I was just glad of the darkness so that he couldn't see the amusement in my eyes. "Do give my best to Daniel, won't you?"

"I will!"

I watched Graham Connors start down the street, the headlamps lining the streets either side illuminating the city of Dublin and I smiled as the light bounced off Graham's balding head. It suited him, though, I always thought.

He reminded me a lot of a young Ben Kingsley - a teenage crush I had once had which had caused me much ribbing from my parents and friends over the years. I hadn't minded, though. I had always found myself drawn to the misunderstood.

Maybe that's what I had found myself drawn to on that night at Cobblestones' when I had first laid eyes on Daniel Sharp.

The way he stared off into space sometimes, looking at nothing in particular, just staring. It unnerved me at times, seeing the man I loved so far away from me, as if he was battling with something inside himself that he couldn't quite voice to those around him.

Maybe that's why he sometimes acted out in the way he did. Maybe he was just misunderstood...

With that thought in my mind, I turned around to see if my husband was waiting for me further down the street, the opposite way to which Graham had gone.

But as I looked around me, there was only the sound of the rush-hour traffic to keep me company, and when fifteen minutes had passed with no more sign of Daniel Sharp - much to my chagrin - I decided to take the bus back home.

It was only a five minute walk from the bus stop to our house, and when I turned the corner to our street, I was surprised to see our familiar little semi was in darkness. It didn't even look like Daniel was at home.

A swell of panic rose within me. What if he had come to meet me, but something dreadful had happened on the way? Of course, monstrous thoughts started to cloud my usually rational judgment, then, and I fumbled in my handbag for my key, opening the solid oak door with a shaking hand.

At the same time as opening my own front door, I heard another door open a few houses down and I looked to my right to see Marina Jimenez standing outside.

"Senora Sharp?" She wrung her hands together in front of her and I noticed a smattering of frown lines appear on her forehead. "Your husband tell you he work tonight, si?"

"I-I'm sorry?" I stayed my key in mid-air as I stared across at Marina, her pretty brown eyes wide on my own. It didn't occur to me in that moment to remember any of the Spanish that she had taught me over the past few months. All I wanted right now was my husband. "I was expecting Daniel to pick me up from..."

"Mummy! Mummy! You're home!"
Suzanna's familiar little squeal alerted me to the fact that I hadn't even thought about my precious little step-daughter since learning of Daniel's decision to leave me stranded in the middle of Dublin.

Guilt made me forget everything then as I bent down to pick up my little girl as she ran towards me, arms out-stretched. It was rare that I got a moment alone with Suzanna, and so I seized the opportunity.

"Marina?" I held Suzanna close to me, relishing the feel of her soft, velvety hair against my cheek. "Thank you for looking after Suzanna. You're a great help to myself and Daniel."

Marina nodded her head towards me, as we both made our way back into our respective homes.

Sure enough, when I stepped inside our comfortable home, I noticed a yellow Post-it stuck to the kitchen countertop.
'Had a call from the University. End of term papers needed grading. Back soon. Love you xx'
Each word - so carefully written in Daniel's own hand - felt like a punch to my stomach. I stood in the open-plan kitchen, silence ringing in my ears as I tried to make sense of the note in my hands.
It didn't make sense. Daniel always did his grading at home in his office. There was no need for him to go into work to do it, and especially not so late in the evening.
"Mummy! Look what Mrs Himmy gave me today!" Suzanna brought me spinning back to the present, her sweet little smile stretching across her cherubic face. I couldn't help but giggle every time she pronounced Marina's surname. "It's a seal! Look! Look!"
"Oh my goodness!" I opened my mouth, feigning the kind of amazement you only ever show to a child who is waving a cuddly toy in your face excitedly. "Suzanna, that is the cutest little seal I have ever seen!"
"It's not real, though, Mummy!" I suppressed a giggle when she looked up at me as if I was just a child myself and I should have known better. "I asked Mrs Himmy for a real one, but she said real seals live by the sea! Is that right, Mummy?"
In that moment, I forced myself to forget about mine and Daniel's date night and I chose, instead, to spend the rest of the evening with my step-daughter.
I dressed Suzanna in her Sesame Street pyjamas and we sat by the fireplace for the rest of the evening, inventing stories about 'Shelly the Seal' and her sea creature friends.
I couldn't remember the last time I had laughed so hard, and by the time I looked at the clock, i was surprised to see It had already struck 9:30pm. Well past Suzanna's bedtime. A bolt of fear struck

through me, knowing that if Daniel walked through the door now, he would never let me near his little girl again.

Well, she was my little girl, as well. He needed to accept that, one day.

"Come on, then, you!" I stood to my feet, stretching my body out like a cat and feeling my tired bones clicking back into place with each twist and turn. "You and Shelly need your rest!"

"Nooo..." Suzanna stuck her bottom lip out comically and I couldn't help but smile at how cute it made her look. On any other child, it might have looked unruly, worthy of a clip around the ear, but not Suzanna. Her cuteness always won me over. "Shelly says no!"

I chuckled as she nuzzled the seals velvety nose against my belly - the highest point on my body she could reach.

"I'll tell you what..." I said, bending down to look at her directly in her big, blue eyes. "If you're a good girl tonight and go to bed like I ask, then, maybe..." I said, reaching out to tickle her ribs and her tinkle of laughter warmed my heart, "Maybe I might ask Daddy to take us somewhere on holiday to see some real seals! What do you think?"

I wasn't prepared for the smile that now spanned Suzanna's cherubic little face. "Really, Mummy! Can we? Really?"

"I don't see why not!"

Suzanna whooped, twirled and danced as the last few embers of the fire crackled beside us. "Did you hear that, Shelly? We're going to see your family!"

I stood in our sitting room, watching our sweet little girl in animated chatter with her new-found friend and smiled at the thought of our first holiday together as a family.

At around 1:15am, I was jolted awake by the sound of a key in the lock. After waiting patiently for a good hour in front of the TV with my glass of red - the light-hearted comedy of both Billy Crystal and Meg Ryan cheering me up somewhat - I had given up waiting and retired to bed.

Bleary-eyed, I stumbled out of bed, pulled on my silk kimono and tip-toed across the landing. Suzanna had become something of a light sleeper in the past few months and I was determined not to wake her.

"Daniel?" I whispered, as I continued my fairy steps down the stairs. "Is that you?"

I heard a slight groan amidst the darkness of the sitting room and when I went to switch on the lamp by the front door, the sight that greeted me made me gasp.

Daniel stood - well, *swayed,* should I say - before me, grinning like a Cheshire Cat as I took in his dishevelled state. He stank of Bourbon and when I took his black, leather coat from him, the smell of cigarettes that emanated from the heavy material made me retch in disgust. I hated the habit.

"Looks like you had a busy night?" I enunciated each word meaningfully, noticing his smile curl to one side as he stumbled over to the sofa. He fell atop of it like a lead weight and I walked straight past him, stopping in the doorway of the sitting room before making my way back upstairs.

I leant against the doorframe, breathing heavily as I tried to control my anger. I knew that if I raised my voice, an explosive argument would surely ensue, and I didn't want to risk waking Suzanna.

"Who *are* you, Daniel Sharp?"

I heard the exasperation in my own voice as I made my way back upstairs.

As my bare feet padded against the plush beige carpets, I was sure that I heard the weary reply escape my husband's lips:

"Miriam, I wish I knew..."

"So, you don't want to call it quits, yet?"
I laughed at my best friend's outspokenness.
"'Course not! What makes you think that?"

We sat in a corner booth at Cobblestones', sharing a pint of Coke. There wasn't many in, judging by the fact that it was 2 'o' clock in the afternoon on a Tuesday, but I was on my lunch break and I was desperate for a catch-up with Sally. It had been at least a couple of months since we had had one of our heart-to-hearts.

"Because you look like Death, hon, that's why!"

"Thanks!" I laughed mirthlessly. "I can always count on you to pay me a compliment!"

"I'm serious, Hel", Sally said, her pretty, green eyes wide on mine. "I don't see you for weeks at a time and when I do, you turn up looking like you've been partying with Led Zeppelin until the early hours of the morning!" She cackled. "What's going on with you?"

I ran my fingers through my greasy hair. I had been too tired to wash it this morning due to Suzanna keeping me up all night with her nasty cold.

"Everything, babe!" I turned my head from side to side, cricking my neck in the process. "It's a never-ending story of Dry-Nites and paperwork at the moment!"

Sally blew air out through her nose, shaking her head in, what looked like, dismay.

"I admire you, Hel! Taking all that on as well as going after a career!" She took a long swig of Coke. "I certainly couldn't have done it!"

I watched my friend absentmindedly, the cogs in my brain turning all of a sudden. "You think I can do it, don't you?"

"What's that?"

"Manage both worlds. Looking after the little one while still pursuing my career?"

Sally shrugged. "Hey, if that's what you want, hon, then go for it!" She took another sip of her Coke. "Besides, Suzanna starts school in September, doesn't she? And you've always got Marina to look after the little'un..."

"I suppose..."

Sally let out a heavy sigh. "Maybe I'm just thinking a little differently now, given my own condition..."

I snapped out of my trance-like state to stare at my friend. A sly smile was tugging at the corner of her mouth in a way that only I could read and I slapped a hand to my mouth. "No! You're not?!"

The curl of her mischievous smile told me everything I needed to know.

"Sally!" I sat back against the plush, red velvet of the booth, hardly able to believe what I was hearing. "When? How? Who?!" The questions fell from my mouth in an almost incoherent slur.

"Hel, this is going to sound awful, but…"

I read my friend's guilty face immediately. "You don't remember anything, do you?" She bit her lip guiltily and I shook my head at her, disapprovingly. "Sally! You can't even remember who?"

"I really don't, hon!" She shook her head, slowly, as if trying to remember. "Hel, I go to a different bar every week, I get drunk off my face, I meet a guy, I take him back to my place and… it always ends the same way! You know me!" She swished her hair to one side, as if she was proud. "Eternal flirt!"

"Oh my Word!" I leant my elbows against the table, my head in my hands. "You are unbelievable!" Sally laughed and I glared across at her. "And by the way, that is not a compliment!" She bit her lip to keep from laughing again. "So, how far along are you?"

Sally merely shrugged as if I'd just asked what she was having for dinner that evening.

"Probably a couple of weeks, I dunno..." She took a hearty sip of Coke before glancing distractedly around the deserted pub. "But I've been puking my guts out every morning for the past few days and so I took a test to be sure, and..." She threw her hands up in the air, that mischievous smile playing on her lips again. "And here I am!"

I stared at her, an incredulous laugh escaping my lips at Sally's blatant devil-may-care attitude to life. "So..." I stared at the grainy wood of the table, wondering what question I was going to ask next. "What are you going to do, Sal?"

"What do you mean?" She looked at me as if I'd said something unforgivable. "I'm keeping the little ruffian, aren't I? I'm not a murderer!"

I sat back again, trying to digest what I had just heard. "This is insane..."

"You'll be there for me, though, won't you, hon?" Sally looked at me, then, and I was surprised to see her usual cheery demeanour shrink slightly into concern. "Through all the squeezing and pushing and epidurals?"

I laughed affectionately at my sweet friend, reaching across the table to take her hand. "Of course I will, babe! I wouldn't miss it for the world!"

A week later, I was still thinking about Sally's shock news.

Daniel and I were sat, snuggled up on the sofa watching a soppy rom-com I couldn't remember the name of, and I nuzzled my head into his neck.

"You alright, baby?"

I felt the pressure of his lips on the crown of my head and I closed my eyes against the tenderness of his touch. My time of the month was about a week away and so my hormones were driving me wild with passion.

Much to my surprise - and delight - things had been going well between us since that dreadful night Daniel had come home in a state of drunken stupor. His apology the next day had been made with extensive grovelling and the tears that had filled his hazel eyes had taken my heart so by surprise that I couldn't help but feel sorry for him.

He had even promised to take us all to Cornwall later in the year so that Suzanna could see the seals for herself. It had been almost a month since then and still, our little girl skipped from room to room as if walking on the clouds themselves.

"I'm feeling great, Daniel..." I sat up on the sofa on all fours, biting my lip teasingly and he grinned at me, his dimples making me even wilder with passion. "In fact, I'd really like to show you how great I'm feeling right now..."

Daniel laughed mischievously, picking up the remote by his side and switching off the TV. It was silent in the house now, except for the crackling of the fire and the beat of my own heart, wild for my husband.

"How much wine have you had tonight, baby?"

I giggled playfully, leaning forward and digging my face into his neck, kissing the skin tenderly as I fiddled with the buttons of his shirt. "I don't need wine, babe..." I said, looking up at him as seductively as I could. "I have you!"

I watched Daniel lean his head back against the sofa, closing his eyes as I began to kiss slowly down his chest, his torso and then, just as I began to undo his zipper...

"Babe, the condoms are in my desk in my office..."

I stayed my eager hands and looked up at him. "Good idea!" I reached up to kiss him hard on the lips. "Another baby probably isn't the wisest idea right now, huh?"

He chuckled as I ran upstairs to his office. Fleetingly, I checked in on Suzanna, smiling as I saw her clutching Shelly tightly to her chest as she slept.

I walked into the office, my eyes scanning the interior. Daniel's office was decorated very formally, the grey walls a little lack-lustre and desperately in need of a fresh lick of paint. His desk sat in the far, left corner and I walked over to it.

Pulling open the drawers one by one, I had no luck in finding what I needed. Just when I felt myself getting frustrated that I wouldn't be able to satisfy my insatiable passion for Daniel, I opened the bottom drawer.

I grinned, biting my lip in pleasure when I found the pack of Trojan's and was just about to close the drawer again, when I found something that caught my eye.

I picked up the photo frame carefully, the beautifully carved silver frame making me gasp in awe.

But when I stared at the woman in the picture, the gasp that fell from my lips surprised even myself.

The woman was certainly not me, of course, and yet her features... I stared at them, my mouth agape, trying to make sense of what I was looking at.

Her baby blue eyes, so similar to mine and Suzanna's, literally stole the air from my lungs. Her white blonde hair - alright - was a little lighter than mine and yet the similarities between us were unmistakable. The wide smile, the unruly blonde curls...

"No..." I quieted the doubts in my mind, refusing to believe them. "You're being ridiculous, Helen!"

"Helen?"

I gasped in alarm and spun around to see Daniel standing in the doorway. I quickly yanked my arm behind my back as if someone had taken me captive and dropped the frame back into the drawer. Daniel was staring hard at me, hazel eyes wide with curiosity.

"What's wrong, baby? Didn't you find them?"

"Right here!" I said, hastily, displaying the pack of Trojan's for him to see. "But, um..." I said, putting two fingers to my head and feigning a headache, "I'm suddenly feeling a little woozy, babe..."

Daniel chuckled, making his way over to me and taking the pack of condoms from my hand with a glint in his eye. "Don't give me that, you little tease!" He cupped my face in his hands and kissed me passionately on the lips. "I'm sure I can convince you..."

And then he nuzzled his own head into my neck and I found myself, once again, giving in to the irresistible charm that was Daniel Sharp.

I turned my back on the saucepan for a moment and leant against the wooden countertop. I hadn't stopped thinking about Sally's pregnancy ever since she'd announced it to me seven months ago and it still played on my mind even now.

"Daniel? Do you ever think about having another baby?"

From where I was watching him sitting on the sofa, his back to me, I was sure I saw him stiffen.

"I think we've got enough on our plate with work at the moment, don't you think?" He stood up from the sofa, walking through the curved alcove into our kitchen. His strong arms wrapped around my waist and I held him close to me.

"Why do you ask, baby?"

"Well", I said, turning around to stir the sauce again, "I'm not saying I'd like one straight away, but...maybe one day? What do you think?"

Daniel was silent for a long time and I wondered, briefly, whether he had heard my question. He started kissing my neck and I shrugged him off playfully. "Daniel, stop it!" I giggled. "Did you hear me?"

He turned me around to face him and he exhaled in a way that reminded me of when I was small and I would ask my father if I could stay up an extra hour before bed. I found it a little condescending, if I was honest.

"To be honest, I've been meaning to ask you something as well, baby." He lowered his head slightly and looked up at me with questioning eyes. I had no idea why he was ignoring such a simple question. "I don't think I can keep Marina on anymore. The monthly expenses seem to be adding up and I don't think I can afford to keep paying her a wage."

I looked up at him, wondering what this had to do with me. "So", I said trying to read the blank expression in his eyes. "What are you asking me, Daniel?"

Daniel rolled his eyes impatiently and I saw the glint of darkness in his eyes again. "Do I have to spell everything out for you? I thought lawyers were smart!"

He laughed and I stared at him, trying to make my frustration evident as I pushed him away with the palm of my hand. "Daniel!"

"Oh, fine!" He took a step back, his hands on his hips in an exaggerated display of authority. "I want you to think about going part-time. Only a couple of hours less each day. You can still earn a decent wage, and you can be there to pick Suzanna up from school at 3:30pm."

I blinked a few times in shock, a smile spreading slowly across my face. "Is this a joke?"

"What do you mean, a joke?" His eyes darkened, and, immediately, I realised my mistake. "You think looking after my daughter is a joke?"

"Of course not!" I defended myself, knowing that this conversation could lead me down a very dangerous path. "You know how much I love Suzanna. But think about what you're asking me, Daniel - I've just started in my role as a paralegal a couple of months ago. What would my boss say if I suddenly said I wanted to reduce my hours? He'd think I was never even serious about the role in the first place!" I stared at my husband, his expression unmoving. "Daniel, you're asking me to sacrifice my entire career! That's not fair!"

"*Fair*?" Daniel's eyes darkened to the point that I felt my heart race in my chest. "I'll tell you what's not fair, Helen!" Daniel slammed the palm of his hand hard against the wooden countertop and I let out a sharp cry of alarm. From somewhere upstairs, I heard a little girl moan in her sleep. "What's not fair, is that every day, I have to look in your eyes and see the image of my dead wife staring back at me!"

I covered my mouth with my hands, almost sinking to the floor with the weight of Daniel's words. They fell upon me, one by one like dominoes, and I tried to make sense of each of them in turn. Like an iron fist to my face, I suddenly remembered the picture I had found in Daniel's office just a few months ago. I looked back up at him in horror.

"That's why you married me, isn't it?" The words were barely audible, even to myself, and I found that I could no longer hold my body off the ground. I sank to the cold, tiled floor in a heap, like a wounded animal. "The picture I saw of her in your drawer..." I gasped for air, trying to make sense of what I had seen all those months ago. "She looked so much like me. Blonde hair, blue eyes...You were trying to recreate your *perfect* little life!" From where I sat on the floor, I looked up at Daniel Sharp with all the strength I had. "You let me fall in love with you!" I sobbed now, unable to stem the piercing pain that shot through my abdomen. "How *could* you?!"

Daniel hadn't moved from where he stood in the middle of the kitchen. I noticed, with a stab to my heart, that his expression hadn't changed. He merely looked annoyed.

"Get up, Helen", he said, as casually as if he was speaking to his daughter. "I don't want Suzanna coming down seeing you like this."

I gritted my teeth, not wanting him to win. I stood up slowly, my gaze fixed on his, spitting each word out in his face. "And I don't want her growing up with a father like you."

I took the slap with as much dignity as I could muster. The force of it stung my cheek and I could feel the burn creeping through my skin painfully.

"You know what?" I plastered on a smile, staring into his eyes that were now cold and calculated and fixed on mine. "I'll accept your offer, Daniel. Of course I'll look after Suzanna." He raised his eyebrows, suddenly interested and I tried my best to keep my voice steady. "I'll make sure that little girl gets all the love and affection she deserves."

"Good." Daniel Sharp appraised me from head to toe as if I was some kind of prize he had won and I curled my lip in sudden disgust. "That's settled, then."

"Daddy?" A little voice rang out from just outside the alcove. "Why is Mummy shouting?"

I drew in a sharp intake of breath at seeing Suzanna's innocent little face looking up at her Dad, adoringly. Her bright blonde Shirley Temple curls were messy around her face and her beautiful, blue eyes were heavy with sleep. All I wanted in that moment was to take her in my arms and keep her safe from the monster in front of me.

But I knew Daniel would never have let me do that. So, instead, I had to watch, silently, as he reached down to pick his little girl up, smiling that familiar smile that had melted my heart on the first moment I had laid eyes on him in Cobblestones'. My heart ached within me at the memory.

"Come on, Baby Blue!" Hearing the significance of that name now nearly made me retch. "Let's get you back to bed and I'll read you a story, shall I?"

I watched, my chest heaving with fear for that precious little girl in front of me, as Daniel turned on his heel and made his way back upstairs with his daughter.

One month later

While I was typing out the minutes from the board meeting, my office phone rang. A part of me prayed it was the police, saying they had found out about my husband's scheming ways and that they were going to lock him up for good. But I knew I was being ridiculous.

"Good morning, Baker & Nesbitt. Helen speaking, how may I..."

"Helen?" A woman's voice called back to me, urgent and wrought with worry. "It's Karen, Sally's mother. She's gone into labour early and she needs you at the hospital with her as soon as you can! Can you get here now, darling?"

Karen Lake sounded desperate and, immediately, I knew what I needed to do. I had promised Sally I would be there for her, no matter what, and I wasn't about to let her down. I threw everything into my little bag and called down from my cubicle to Fiona Smith, sitting at the reception desk.

"Fiona, tell Mr Baker I'm taking the rest of the day off, will you?" Fiona looked at me running towards the door, puzzled. "My best friend's just gone into labour!"

"Will do!" She called after me. "Hope it goes well!"

I needed to stop by the house quickly before I went to the hospital, as I had bought a couple of warm blankets for the baby. They were still at the back of my closet.

I ran into the house, barely noticing Daniel sitting on the sofa watching TV, the familiar Countdown clock sounding in my ears.

"Going somewhere?"

"Don't ever talk to me again, Daniel", I said, as calmly as I could. "I'll be filing for a divorce first thing tomorrow, so expect the next few months to be rather busy for us, *darling*."

"She's a little early, isn't she? Sally, I mean."

My right leg froze on the stair and I slowly walked backwards a little until I was standing in the doorway to the living room. I narrowed my eyes at him. "How did you know?"

Daniel shrugged, standing up and making his way over to the fridge. "Her mother called just now. Karen, is it?" He took a bottle of Corona from the top shelf and popped the cap using his teeth, slamming the fridge door shut. "I did tell her to be more careful with the booze, that night, you know. Never knew when to call it quits, that one..."

"Daniel?" I made my way over to him, slowly, as if I was the predator and he was the prey. I wasn't afraid of Daniel Sharp anymore. He had done enough to hurt me, already... "What are you talking about?"

"What do you mean?" He stared at me, genuinely surprised. "Sally didn't tell you? I would have thought she'd told you all the juicy details about the night I knocked her up?"

I didn't know what happened to me, then. All I saw was red. "Why, you *piece* of...!"

I flung myself at him like a coil released and I felt his large hands clamp around my wrists. I screamed in agony as he threw me to the floor like a rag doll and I fell in a heap to the hardwood floor.

I laid on the ground, trying to regain my breath as I heard his footsteps padding against the wooden floor, and then the squeak of leather as he sat back down.

Like a blow to the head, thoughts of that Wednesday evening eight months ago came spiralling back to me; Daniel coming home late from work, dishevelled and reeking of whisky and cigarettes; the suspicious smear of a coral-coloured pigment lining his collar. The anger I now felt was white hot, searing in my veins so that I knew I needed to escape, afraid that if left in Daniel Sharps presence any longer, I would not be able to prevent myself from tightening my hands around his neck and...

"Daddy, Daddy! Look at my drawing!"

I heard the gentle thud-thud of little feet on the landing and the excited squeal of a little girl making her way downstairs to her father.

"You won't get away with this, Daniel..." The break in my voice gave away my fear - not of Daniel - but of my precious little stepdaughter and I stood up slowly, dusting myself down with trembling hands. "If you hurt that little...."

"Look, Daddy! I drew the beach and the sea and the sun, and..." Suzanna flew through to the sitting room in a beautiful flurry of golden curls and huge, blue eyes. She was waving a crumpled piece of white A4 paper - awash with an assortment of bright yellows and blues - in her fathers face and I felt tears prick my eyes in an instant.

Her innocence was so pure, her experience of life still so untouched that I had never wanted to take her in my arms so desperately and free her of the darkness that now trapped her. Even if she was still so blissfully unaware that it was now staring her in the face...

"Baby Blue, that's beautiful!" I clenched my jaw tight, gripping the edge of the kitchen countertop for support as I watched Daniel take his daughter onto his lap, planting a tender kiss on her dewy forehead and stroking her golden curls away from her face in a gesture of fatherly love.

It was all I could do not to scream in justifiable rage at my husbands twisted range of emotions...

"Mummy, why are you crying?" I looked up to see Suzanna staring at me with her huge, baby blue eyes - so similar to my own - and my heart ached for her.

"I'm alright, sweetheart, I was just..."

"Mummy was just popping out to get some sweeties for tonight! Weren't you, Mummy?"

With his back still turned, Daniel barely moved his head to glance in my direction. I wanted to believe it was his shame from preventing him doing so, but I knew I was just kidding myself.

"Yep", I said, curtly. "I'll be back soon, sweetheart, and we can all watch a film together. Would you like that?"

Suzanna grinned at me, and I watched - my heart full - as she clapped her little hands together in childish glee.

"Yes! Yes! Can I come with you, Mummy?"

I opened my mouth to speak, but Daniel beat me to it. "Why don't we pick out a film now while Mummy goes and gets the sweeties?" Daniel bounced Suzanna on his knee and she squealed in delight. "Mummy will be back soon, won't you?"

"Of course...", I said, my heart now so heavy in my chest that I could almost feel my body sagging in defeat, the kitchen countertop now no longer a sufficient support for my breaking heart. "I promise I'll be as quick as I can, sweetheart..."

I spoke too quietly for them to hear me, though, and, with all the strength I had left in my weakened body, I walked out the open door, vowing to keep the promise I had made to my precious little step-daughter.

Chapter 5

Suzy, Cornwall, 2015

I put my head between my knees, staring down at the smooth, flat surface of the rock underneath me.

I wanted to vomit. There was just too much for me to take in that I needed to let out as much anger and confusion and shock as I possibly could.

"I just don't understand…" I drew in a shuddering breath, my hands clasped tightly on my knees as if steeling myself for what was about to come. But nothing happened.

And then I felt the gentle touch of my mother's hand on my arm.

"Suzanna?" There was a sob in her voice. "Please look at me, sweetheart! I need to ask you something…"

With all the effort I could manage, I turned my head to the side and met my mother's penetrating gaze. I had never seen her look as raw as she did in that moment. "Did he ever hurt you, Suzanna? Did he…"

"No! Never!" I exclaimed, discerning the meaning behind her words and I started to sob loudly. I couldn't hold it in any longer. "He would never have…"

"It's alright, sweetheart." I felt my mother's hand rubbing my back soothingly, and a memory flooded back to me of her doing the same thing when I was five years old. "I always knew he loved you unconditionally. It was what I loved most about him."

I sobbed, leaning my head on my mother's shoulder and suddenly realising I had never embraced my mother of my own accord. Her hand around my shoulder felt oddly comforting, all of a sudden. "How could I not have known? All these years!" I brought a hand to my mouth to stem a cry of anguish. "How could I not have known who he was?"

We were silent, listening to the waves beating against the rocks, calmer now. The sky had darkened above us and I could see St Michael's Mount from the corner of my eye; a great fortress of solitude that I suddenly felt a desperate need to run to.

"I spoke to the coroner after we received the autopsy results…" My mother's voice was oddly calm against my ear, and I suddenly felt a surge of renewed admiration for her fierce spirit. "They said that they found bottles of medication – plural – scattered at the side of his bed."

"What kind?"

My mother looked at me, then, and her eyes were full of motherly concern.

"Are you sure you want to hear all of this, Suzanna?"

"Of course I'm sure!" I spoke, a little too sharply, although angry nonetheless. "Everything I thought I knew about him was a lie that he let me believe! I need to know!" I sobbed. "Please!"

My mother breathed in deeply, closing her pretty eyes – so similar to mine – as if preparing herself for her next few words. "Suzanna, your father suffered from Bipolar Disorder for many years…" she began, and I felt my heart tighten at the shock revelation. "He had being seeing a therapist in the last couple of years who even said he showed signs of IED. It stands for Intermittent Explosive Disorder." I stared at her, her words sliding over my head in confusion. "One minute, he was the life and soul of the party, the next…" I watched my mother's face slip from admiration to fear in just one second. "The next, he was wishing I was dead…"

A sob rose in her throat and I held my mother in my arms, wishing the sea would wash over us and erase the pain that lingered within us both. "Did he ever even tell you?"

I felt my mother shake her head against my shoulder and I let out a heavy sigh.

"I loved your father so much, Suzanna!" She pulled away from me then, and I watched her tears fall from her eyes like rain. She didn't even bother to wipe them away. "But he was only in love with a memory! A memory that he never forgot until the day he died!"

"I'm so sorry, Mum…" I sobbed as my mother held my cheek in the palm of her hand. "If I had known…"

"Sweetheart, there was nothing you could have done." She wiped a tear from the end of my nose with her thumb. "You were just a child."

I closed my eyes, listening to the deafening rush of the sea below us and suddenly recalling a thousand different memories all at once.

"He told me things about you…" I whispered. "Horrible things. Things I didn't even understand at the time."

"I know…"

"Graham?" I said, noticing my mother's eyes cloud over and I remembered the kindness that Graham had shown me at the airport just a few days before, willing me to take my mother's side, even then. "He told me that you had an affair with him, and that…" I swallowed hard, forming the words on my tongue painfully, "…you wanted to leave us both because you didn't love us anymore! I was only six years old!"

I saw the pain flash through her blue eyes, but she dismissed it, bravely.

"There were so many times that I wanted to tell you the truth, sweetheart. The truth about your father, about who your real mother was. That day I left the house, I rang social services straight away." My mother looked at me, her blue eyes pleading my forgiveness. "I had to, Suzanna. I was so worried that he would…"

"Mum, stop. Please." My tears fell onto the rock beneath us - a solid support for our crumbling grief. "I understand", I said, even though the thought of that my father could ever be violent towards another human being - to me - made me feel sick to my stomach.

"They visited the house every day for about two weeks", my mother continued. I watched her eyes searching the horizon, as if the answers she were seeking were just beyond. "They even asked to speak with your nanny - Marina - but Daniel informed them she had left for Spain a few days before and she hadn't given him an address so there was no way of getting in touch." I watched my mother as she chewed at her lip, remembering every detail in her mind. "I always suspected Marina sensed some strain between Daniel and I in the months leading up to the divorce. Maybe if she hadn't left, then there might have been a chance that..."

I heard the break in my mother's voice and I reached out to squeeze her hand that was shaking against the sodden rock.

"I know you're hurting, Mum, and I am so sorry that I was never there for you when you needed me..." I said, hearing the break in my own voice and clearing my throat meaningfully, "But, I need you to know that in all my twenty-seven years of living with him, my father never laid a hand on me. He never hurt me and he never gave me any reason to fear for my safety. You need to know that, Mum."

My mother exhaled - a shaky breath that she blew out gently through pursed lips - and a swell of affection for the woman in front me, the woman I had thought I had known everything about, took me quite by surprise.

"I'm very happy to hear that, Suzanna." My mother smiled thinly at me, her stoic manner despite the circumstances never ceasing to amaze me. We both hugged our legs tighter to our chests as we stared out at the darkening horizon, and I sensed in that moment a tie being formed between my mother and I that was growing stronger with every second..

"It seemed that he was only ever himself when it was just you and him." She curled a strand of beautiful ashen hair behind her ear, and I noticed a smattering of silver hairs that had begun to show around her temples. "You two had a bond that, I admit, I always envied. And I suppose that's what Social Services noticed as well. They saw a father that absolutely doted on his daughter, and, soon enough, my case against him was closed. Besides", she continued, and I was sure I could hear the slight edge to her voice. "there was never any evidence that Daniel was ever violent towards me. And I have to say," she said, a dry laugh escaping her lips, "I was a little annoyed that the bruises on my wrists never showed!"

My mother must have seen the discomfort in my features as her hard expression softened on my own. "Oh, sweetheart, I'm sorry, I didn't mean to..."

"It's alright", I said, struggling to equate the loving father I had grown up with to the passive-aggressive, troubled man my mother had known. "I suppose it's just going to take a while until..."

"Of course it will, sweetheart. I understand."

Somewhere above us, I heard the relaxed chatter of a man and woman walking along the path, and I looked over at my mother. She was tilting her head back against a slight breeze and I couldn't help but smile at the weight I could see lifting from her shoulders. She looked lighter, somehow.

"I went to stay with Sally for a while afterwards, helped her look after the baby."

I stared across at my mother in unbridled shock. "You looked after the woman that had given birth to your husbands child?"

"Suzanna, Sally was my best friend." My mother looked at me, her eyes fixed on mine and I felt like a child being disciplined. "We'd known each other all our lives. I wasn't going to suddenly abandon her when she needed me. Besides", she said, another dry laugh escaping coral-coloured lips, "Sally's a terrible liar! When I forced Daniel to take a DNA test and she found out that he was the father, the look of genuine horror and remorse in her eyes was enough for me to know what she thought of him. Goodness knows how much she had had to drink that night..."

I tried to laugh but the sound came out hollow. Even after all my mother had told me, Daniel Sharp was still my father and I had loved him.

"I tried to visit you every chance I got, sweetheart", she continued, her words flowing now like the waves beneath us. "But as you got older, he became more and more protective of you and then, as soon as I left for Foxrock after the divorce, he hardly ever let me see you." I noticed her bottom lip quiver slightly. "He was a very sick man, Suzanna. Remember that, please…"

My mother was silent by my side and I inhaled slowly, letting the sea breeze tangle my curly hair into even more knots.

"Mum?" I stared out to sea, noticing lights on the horizon. I guessed it must have been one of the boats returning to the harbour just a few metres away. "Did you want to stay in Mousehole a little longer? I can always…"

"No, no. You don't need to do that. Besides, you don't have enough room for me." I noticed her smile slyly. "Think about all the make-up I've brought… That'd take up at least your entire bathroom!"

I laughed, for the first time in a long time.

Slowly, as if it pained us both to do so, we stood up against the rock, beginning the short descent back down to the path. It was almost dark now, the outline of the little boat on the horizon getting dimmer by the minute. "So", I said, inhaling deeply as we walked back along the coastal path. I glanced sideways at my mother. "I suppose I should give Graham a second chance, now, huh?"

My mother sighed deeply, and I heard the love in her voice. I was happy for her. Graham was a good man, I had always known that. I had just been blinded by so many of my father's lies over the years that it had impaired my ability to trust anyone. I hated him for that. "He's stuck with me through everything, that man."

"I'm happy for you, Mum." I nudged her as we mounted the little flight of stone steps back up to the street. "You deserve it."

My mother smiled at me, kissing me on the cheek, and a thought suddenly popped into my mind.

If Sally Lake really had given birth to my father's child, then that meant I had a half-sibling hiding away somewhere, surely?

I opened my mouth to speak, but my mother had already started down the path towards the harbour and I chose, instead, to revel in the new-found relationship I had just formed with the woman in front of me.

My wonderful, brave step-mother.

Chapter 6

I sat back against our little peach sofa in our apartment, trying to digest everything my mother had just unleashed upon me. She had gone back to the hotel in Penzance later that day, promising to ring me the moment she was back to arrange another visit for a few weeks' time. In fact, a part of me wanted to return to Ireland with her.

"I can't believe it, I really just can't believe it..." Fran was saying, over and over, her gaze fixed on a copy of the Radio Times that sat on our little coffee table. She looked up at me, pretty hazel eyes wide. "Everything?"

"Everything!" I repeated. I looked up at the skylight, noticing a couple of stars shining in the darkening sky. "Everything was a lie!"

Fran blew air out through her mouth in disbelief, and it sounded just like the rush of the waves outside our little apartment.

"Are you alright, Baby Bl...?" Fran's voice cut off so sharply that I looked across at her, her face ripening pink. "Sorry, babe, I didn't mean..."

"It's alright, Fran." I said, placing my hand on top of her knee in reassurance. "I'm still trying to absorb everything myself."

We sat in silence for a while and I stared, blankly, at the TV screen. Fran had muted it as soon as I had walked in, seeing my face had turned a ghostly pale. I watched the news reporter's lips moving and I tried to figure out if I could decipher what she was saying to try and distract myself. But my brain was wired too tightly to function and I let my head sink back against the sofa again, exhausted.

"Did you want a tea, babe?"

I was just about to politely decline Fran's tea request, when I heard a phone vibrate loudly. I reached in my own pocket, but I saw Fran do the same.

"Sorry, it's mine, babe."

I watched as her thumb moved quickly over her phone, her pretty, freckled face a picture of concentration as she typed. "Looks serious", I said, with a chuckle. "Who is it?"

"My mum", she said, pressing Send and shoving the phone back in her pocket. Her little denim shorts hugged the tops of her thighs and she tucked her long legs to one side. "She's been away in Devon for a week visiting a friend, so I said she could pop round for a bit..." She looked at me, guilt suddenly registering as if she'd said something she shouldn't have. "That's alright, isn't it, babe?"

"'Course it is!" I stood up, making my way over to the kitchen to boil the kettle. "It'll be nice to see your Mum again. It's been ages since I saw her!"

"Awesome!" I turned back to Fran, flicking through the pages of the Radio Times. "So, let's see what rubbish is on the box to watch tonight!"

About thirty minutes later, I heard a knock at the door.

"Can you get that, babe?" I heard Fran shout from downstairs. "I'm on the loo!"

I laughed, throwing our copy of the Radio Times onto the coffee table in haste and padded downstairs in my comfortable slippers.

Opening the door wide, I saw Valerie Rice standing in front of me, looking as stunning as ever.

"Hi, Valerie!" I said, standing to one side to let her in. "How are you?"

Valerie walked through the door, rubbing her manicured hands together and bringing them to her full lips, blowing air between them.

"Glad to be back home!" She laughed dryly, removing her coat and placing it on the coat rack next to me as if she had lived here all her life. "How are you, anyway, hon?"

She turned to me, stunning green eyes wide on mine. Her hair, a natural shade of auburn, just like Fran's, fell in waves around her shoulders and I couldn't help but notice how attractive she was at forty-eight.

"I could be better", I said, honestly and Valerie looked at me, concerned. "What's wrong, hon?"

"It's a long story!" I started to ascend the stairs just as Fran came out the bathroom. "You don't want to know, believe me!"

"Mum!" Fran ran over to her mother, squeezing her tight. "How was your holiday?"

I pulled up a chair from our little dining table, setting it by our little two-seater sofa.

"Cold and wet! That's what!" Valerie sat down heavily onto our sofa next to me, crossing her shapely thighs. "Chris and I hardly left the apartment all week!"

"Mum, that's gross!" Fran screwed her face up in disgust, pouring water into three mugs. "I really didn't need to know that!"

Valerie cackled and I couldn't help but laugh at her candid manner. "I didn't mean that, baby!" She ran her gold-painted talons through her hair, stopping half-way with a sly smile. "Although, now you mention it…"

I laughed aloud just as Fran came over with our teas and looked up at my best friend's face, her pretty face pinched in disgust. "You are far too honest, sometimes, Mum, it's disgusting!"

Valerie cackled again, taking a sip of her tea. "You must get it from somewhere, baby?" She turned to me, green eyes twinkling. "Am I right, Suzy?"

I laughed into my tea, just as I heard a vibration.

Fran and I looked at one another, reading each other's mind telepathically. "That wasn't me this time, babe!"

I reached into my own pocket to retrieve my phone and my heart stopped when I saw the name on my home screen.

"Who is it?" Fran stared at me, reading my shocked expression. "Is it…"

"Justin." I swallowed hard, scanning the miss-spelt words and feeling my heart ache inside me. "He wants to meet up."

"A boy?" Valerie let out a dramatic sigh, reading the pain between my words. "What has he done, Suzy?"

"Nothing, it's just…" I glanced across at her, wondering how she could be such a good judge of character. "I don't know what he…"

"He dumped her, Mum!" I exhaled sharply in defeat at Fran's abrupt end to the conversation. "He dumped her without any explanation or any care for her feelings!" Fran sat down on the dining room chair, staring at me meaningfully. "He's an idiot, is what he is, Suzy!"

"I know, I just can't help but wonder…"

"Listen to me, hon", Valerie lifted one leg up onto the sofa and turned to me, taking my hand in hers. I stared at her curiously. "If he wants to meet up with you and you haven't seen this boy since he so callously dumped you", she emphasised, and I couldn't help but smile at the fury in her pretty eyes, "you need to do the noble thing and put this to rest. In your heart, and your mind."

I stared at her, narrowing my eyes at her. "And how do I do that, exactly?"

"You find out why", she said, so simply it made me wonder whether she had been through the same situation at my age. "You find out why he's being an idiot, and then you move on." She flashed her white teeth at me comically. "Simples!"

"Simples!" Fran repeated, laughing at her mother's words of wisdom and I shook my head in wonder, taking a long gulp of tea.

"Then, Mrs Rice", I said, plastering on my bravest smile, "that's what I'll do!"

I texted Justin back about an hour later. Not straight away, of course. I didn't want him thinking I was sat by my phone for the past two weeks, pining for him.

"Where are you meeting him?"

The next morning, Fran sat on the edge of the bed, watching me apply my make-up meticulously. I hated myself for worrying so much about how I looked in front of him, but I needed him to see this whole break-up had not caused me to wallow in my grief. I didn't want him thinking I had morphed into Morticia from the Adams Family.

I rubbed in my foundation, giving myself a healthy glow and applied the kohl and mascara I now swore by.

"The Boatshed, on Wharf Road?" I said, widening my eyes and letting out a cry of pain as I poked myself in the eye with my mascara stick. "You know it?"

"M-hmm." Fran sighed, dreamily. "Josh took me there on our third date."

I ran my fingers through my curls, shaking them out the best I could for extra volume. I turned around to face my best friend, hands on my hips as confidently as I could manage.

"What do you think?"

"H-O-T, hot, as always, babe!" She grinned, winking at me in my dark, denim trousers and stripy black-and-white V-neck. "And make sure the idiot knows what he's been missing!"

I sat at a corner table in The Boatshed, waiting to see if I could see Justin making his way down the Promenade.

I jumped suddenly when a plump, red-headed waitress appeared at my side.

"Want anything, sweetheart?"

"Um..." I bit my lip, thinking, noticing I hadn't even looked at the menu yet. "Can I have five more minutes, please?"

The plump waitress nodded silently, placing her pen and pad back in her dress pocket and leaving me alone again.

I picked up the menu and scanned through the options. I wasn't hungry in the slightest but I felt self-conscious all of a sudden, and I pretended to read for a few minutes.

Nearly jumping out of my skin when I felt a tap on the window next to me, I turned to see Justin Wright waving at me flirtatiously through the window. Despite myself, my heart fluttered at seeing him again, and I cursed under my breath.

I smiled, gesturing for him to come inside, and waited, heart racing slightly at what I was sure would be quite a tense conversation. A loud voice in my head shouted at me to run, but I quickly dismissed it.

"Suzy!" His husky voice, so familiar, made my heart ache as he sat down opposite me. "How have you been?"

I stared at him now, taking in his long mane of golden hair that fell to his shoulders. He had deep brown eyes, setting off a deeply tanned complexion that I had always found myself swooning at whenever I was in his company. A true surfer dude, I had fallen in love with his free-spiritedness and zest for life.

Justin was grinning, which I thought was strange. Fran had told him about my father's funeral, hadn't she? And if he had truly felt regret about our recent separation, then wouldn't he at least look a little bit more upset?

"Not great, seeing as I've just lost my father, Justin..." I said, a little irritated that he hadn't even asked about the funeral.

"Oh, Jeez, I totally forgot, Suzy!" He took my hand in his and I tried to swallow the lump that was rising in my throat. "Are you alright?"

"I'm fine", I lied, praying that I could keep a tight lid on my emotions throughout the rest of this conversation. "So, how are you?"

"So-so..." he said, and then I noticed, with maybe a little bit too much glee, his face fall slightly. "I've missed you, Suzy." I looked down at the salt-and-pepper shakers distractedly, wondering what to say next. "I miss being with you."

"I miss you, too..." I said, unable to look at him directly in the eye, a lump beginning to form in my throat.

"Listen, Suzy..." he said, folding his muscled arms against the table and all I wanted to do was reach forward and feel his familiarly warm touch against mine.

"When I said what I said a few weeks back..." *Two weeks back*, I said, silently to myself. "I wasn't thinking straight. I had an argument with my father just a few hours before, and..." he inhaled slowly, and I waited with bated breath, "I took my anger out on you. I'm sorry, babe."

"Justin", I said, frowning at him, "you can't just dump someone because you're angry about something! Do you know how callous that is?"

"Suzy, I know that, and I'm sorry!" He reached across the table, taking my hand in his and I let myself sink into his touch. Warm, and strong. "Forgive me, please. I need you. I want you…"

I stared at him for a long while, wondering whether to trust my head or my heart. "I don't know, Justin", I looked out of the window at the crowds of people walking up and down the Promenade, and, fleetingly, I remembered when I was here with my mother and father all those years ago. I felt sick, all of a sudden. "You really hurt me…"

"I know, babe." I turned back to him, and he cupped my cheek with his hand. It was hot against my skin and I felt my heart race, thinking about all the times we had been together. "Let me prove how much you mean to me." He grinned at me, teasingly, and his crooked smile made my heart pound. "Tonight, at mine after the beach party? I'll wine and dine you! What do you say?"

I stared at him, long and hard, trying to see if I could detect any hint of malice in his eyes. I wondered, briefly, if my mother had done that the first time she had laid eyes on my father. "This is your last chance, Justin! If you screw up…"

"I won't, babe!" He pulled me forwards, kissing me tenderly on the lips and I gave him a small, tentative smile. "I promise!"

I took a deep breath, feeling hungry all of a sudden.

"So, shall I order something for us?" He drummed his hands against the table, a habit he always did when he was impatient. "I'm famished!"

"I think I'll have a BLT…" I mused, looking at the menu again.

"Coming up!"

Justin got up from his chair and made his way over to the counter to order.

The waitress had clearly forgotten all about me…

I turned back to look out the window, and, as I did, I noticed Justin's phone screen light up. He had left it on the table.

Glancing back, I noticed Justin rolling off our orders to the waitress behind the counter. Reaching my hand over, I slid his phone towards me, reading the message on the home screen.

Really enjoyed last night, sweety! You were amazing! ;)

See you at the beach party tonight… xxx

I let out a gasp of anguish, feeling like I had been stabbed through with a sword. In fact, I think that would have hurt less.

I stood up sharply, picking up my jacket and storming out of The Boatshed, hearing Justin's voice calling after me in confusion.

"I don't need this right now, Fran!" I sobbed against my best friend, my tears flowing thick and fast. "I've barely been able to cope with the news about my father, and now this?"

"I know, babe, I'm so sorry…" She stroked my head that was tucked against her shoulder and I found I could hardly control my breathing. "He's such an idiot!"

"I didn't want to get back with him, Fran, I didn't…" I sobbed, feeling like a child in Fran's arms; pathetic and vulnerable. "It's just that he was so convincing, I really believed that he wanted to be with me! How could I have been so stupid?"

"Hon, that's men for you!" I heard creaky footsteps at the side of me, and I sat up, surprised to see Valerie Rice was still here. I wiped my eyes hastily, embarrassed. "You've got to be a mind-reader sometimes to know what they're thinking!" She let out her now-famous cackle, going over to the kitchen and helping herself to a beer from the fridge. "And they think that we're bad!"

"Babe", Fran said, decidedly, clasping my hand in hers. "What you need to do now is throw yourself back into work and forget all about him. I know that's easier said than done, but the sooner you do that, the better!"

I stared at Fran, her sympathetic face making me want to hug her and never let go.

"I know…" I said, letting out a shuddering breath. "I know."

"Like I said, hon", Valerie said, taking a swig from her beer bottle as well as any man, "now you know why he's an idiot, you can move on!"

I chuckled through my tears, noticing little spots of darker denim on my jeans where my tears had fallen. "You're right", I said, sighing. "You're always right, Valerie!"

"'Course I am, hon!"

I felt my phone vibrate again in my pocket and I let out a loud growl of frustration.

"If this is who I think it is…" But I stopped halfway through my sentence, as I read the text on my phone. "It's my mum." I frowned at the message, noticing everyone in the room had fallen silent. "She's a couple of hours away from boarding the plane back home and wants to know whether me and Fran want to join her for a girl's holiday in Ireland?"

Fran let out a surprised laugh. "Is she feeling alright? It's not like your mother to be so spontaneous, is it?"

"Sounds like a great idea, I'd say!" Valerie chimed in, her green eyes widening as she curled a tendril of coppery hair behind her ear. "Would she let me join?"

Fran and I laughed, bemused at my mother's offer. I turned to my best friend and raised my eyebrows, questioningly. "What do you think?"

I could see Fran thinking about the offer, her hazel eyes meeting her mother's questioningly. "I could do with a break, to be honest!"

"That's the spirit, hon!" Her mother grinned, turning to me, all of a sudden. "Ask your mother if I can join, too, will you, Suzy? It is a girly holiday, after all!"

"Mum!" Fran stared at her mother, incredulous. "You can't just invite yourself like that! Helen doesn't even know you!"

"Oh, don't be daft!" She waved a manicured hand in the air. "You know me, darling! We'll be firm friends by the end of the holiday, you wait and see!"

Chapter 7

The three of us arrived at Newquay airport at 3:30pm and I searched the check-in area for any sign of my mother. The four check-in queues were long and I searched each one, standing on my tip-toes to see if I could locate her.

"Can you see her anywhere?"

Suddenly, Fran spoke up. "That's her, isn't it?"

She was pointing to the second queue, and, immediately, I noticed her. She was wearing the same jeans as yesterday, with a red sweater that hugged her waist snugly. Her light, ash hair was curled this time, like mine, and I smiled at seeing her.

"Mum!"

I saw my mother turn around and her face crumpled from one of pensiveness to sheer delight. "Suzanna!" I kissed her on the cheek and she took my little suitcase from me, propping it up against her own. "I didn't think you'd come!"

"Hey, Mrs Connors!"

"Francesca?" My mother stared at my best friend in unbridled shock. Her bright blue eyes were wide. "It's so nice to see you again!"

I noticed my friend blush coyly and I couldn't help but smile at her genuineness. "And you!" She turned to her own mother, introducing her politely. "This is my mother, Valerie Rice."

"Nice to meet you, Valerie!" I watched as my mother extended her hand out towards Fran's mother, appraising Valerie Rice oddly, I noticed. "Will you be joining us?"

"I was told I'm allowed!" Valerie cackled and I bit my lip from laughing at her brazen attitude. "Is that alright, Helen?"

They stared at each other, and, all of a sudden, I felt like I was in the middle of a western, watching two cowboys about to duel in the middle of a town.

And then I saw a gentle smile break out on my mother's face and I immediately relaxed. "Of course it is!" She grinned, placing a hand on Valerie's arm affectionately. "The more the merrier!"

We waited in line to be checked in, and as I chatted casually with my own mother, I heard Valerie whisper to her daughter behind us; "Told you!"

We arrived at Dublin airport at around 4:45pm and I felt a sudden wave of déjà vu wash over me.

I hadn't even been back in Cornwall a week and, yet, here I was, back where I started. I didn't know whether to feel elated that I was here with my mother and my best friend, or a little nauseated that my memories of this country were now tainted.

"Suzy?" I felt my mother's hand on my arm as we walked through the double doors. She had said that Graham would be waiting somewhere outside with the car to take us to Foxrock. "Thank you for agreeing to this, sweetheart. I really need this, you know, just to put everything behind us and move on." Her eyes were intent on mine, as if we were the only ones in the entire airport. "You understand that, don't you?"

I smiled widely, understanding completely. "Why do you think I agreed?"

She grinned just as there was a loud honk of a car horn.

"You lot going to stand there all day, or are you getting in?" Graham leaned over the passenger side, his handsome smile lighting up his eyes. "Girls holiday starts now, doesn't it?"

I heard Valerie's cackle behind us. "Got yourself a good'un, there, haven't you, Helen?"

"I'll say!"

I was surprised at how quickly Valerie and my mother had bonded. They had chatted easily on the plane as if they'd known each for years and I was silently relieved - it had been a long time since I had seen my mother this happy.

"Hey, Suzy?" Fran nudged me, whispering in my ear as we fell into a heap in the back seat. "Maybe we'll bump into Kevin!"

I glared across at her, smiling, and hoping that she couldn't see the guilty blush creeping up my cheeks.

Graham ground the car to a gentle halt against the gravel driveway of 206 Aintree.

I opened the car door, stepping out and looking up at the house now in a whole new light.

To my mother, this house had become a safe haven of love, peace and warmth. Three things that my father had never shown her.

"This place is ridiculous!" Fran exclaimed, her hands on her hips as she looked up at the grandeur of 206 Aintree.

My mother glared across at her and I couldn't help but laugh out loud. "She means it's amazing, Mum!" I said, decoding my best friend's choice of words.

"You young'un's nowadays!" My mother laughed and it was such an unfamiliar sound that I couldn't help but smile. She looked so pretty when she smiled. "You make me feel ancient!"

We all laughed but it was Valerie's cackle that drowned all of us out. "How do you think I feel, then, Helen? I'm a year older than you!"

"Hey!" Graham stepped out of the car, his grey, tailored suit making him look like something out of an Armani advert. "You two stop talking about age! You're making me feel like the dinosaur of the group!"

All four of us burst out laughing then as Graham led us through the front door of their stately home in the country.

Fran and I lounged across my mother's three-seater sofa in the spacious living room, relishing the feel of her beige fabric cushions against our faces.

We both laid on our sides facing the TV – mounted on their huge, statement wall that displayed an image of the New York skyline. My mother had certainly put her own stamp on this house, I could tell.

"Why couldn't they have provided cushions like this on the plane?"

I giggled at Fran, lying on the opposite side of the sofa, her feet playing with my own as we lay like book ends on the comfortable sofa. "I would have fallen asleep in seconds!"

"Tell me about it!" I sighed, nuzzling my own head into the comfortable fabric. "This is blissful!"

"Girls?" I blinked my eyes open to see Valerie Rice standing in the doorway, manicured nails tapping the doorframe seductively. "Prosecco or Rose?"

"Rose!" Fran and I chimed in unison and we laughed. "Coming up, my dears!"

When Valerie left the room, I listened to her voice – audible, I was sure, from at least a mile away – echoing down from the kitchen. My mother was laughing and I heard the loud pop of a cork, followed swiftly by even more laughter. I closed my eyes, smiling to myself at my mother's sudden change of character. It was as if, all these years, she had been carrying her dark secret within her, and now, finally releasing it to the world, she was able to let go. I couldn't even begin to imagine how that felt for her.

I closed my eyes, smiling and wondering what the future now held for me and my mother. A woman I had thought I had known everything about...

I jolted awake at the sound of the doorbell, the long, melodic tone light and comforting.

"I'll get it!" Fran jumped up from her chair, auburn waves bouncing behind her back as she did. "If I don't get up soon, I'll be asleep before I know it!"

I giggled to myself as she sprang out the room, knowing that someone like Fran could never stay still for too long.

I closed my eyes again without a shred of guilt, hearing the creak of the oak door as it was opened wide.

"Hey, um... Is Mrs Connors at home?"

The man's voice sounded familiar, I thought, as I strained my ears.

"Mrs Connors!" Fran shouted down the hall towards the kitchen. "Some guy's at the door for you!"

I laughed at my best friend, the likeness between her and her mother suddenly obvious to me in that moment.

I heard the sound of my mother's kitten heels against the hardwood floor and then her voice, much softer than Fran's; "Kevin!" My heart did an odd sort of flip at the sound of the name and I froze against the sofa. "How are you doing, sweetheart?"

Just then, Fran came back in the room and her pretty, hazel eyes were wide on mine. "That's Kevin?" she mouthed to me, gesturing a thumb back towards the door. "He's hot!"

I stared at her meaningfully, already feeling the heat rise against my cheeks.

"Not great, to be honest…"

I tried my hardest to listen to the conversation just outside the door, all the while feeling Fran nudge me like a naughty teenager and silently scolding her for it.

"She moved back to her parents' yesterday, so it's been pretty hard…" I heard him say quietly and I strained to hear. "I suppose it's going to take a while, until…"

His voice broke and I heard my mother's voice, calm and soothing. "Oh, Kevin, I understand. I'm so sorry, sweetheart."

I looked over at Fran and her eyes were wide on mine. I knew, immediately, that we were both thinking the same thing. Surely, Kevin wasn't talking about…?

"Why don't you come in for a little bit, eh?" I heard my mother offer and I felt my heart race a little. "We're pouring some wine as we speak! The girls have just come up from Cornwall, so you can say hello, if you like?"

"Suzy and Fran are here?"

Fran nudged me so hard then that I let out a sharp yelp of pain.

"Suze?"

Just then, Kevin appeared in the doorway and I froze, despite myself.

"Kevin?"

"What are you doing back so soon?" He leant against the doorframe, dressed casually in a navy blue shirt against green khaki combats. It suited his bulky frame perfectly and I couldn't help but notice the way his dark hair curled around his ears. Fran was right, I thought, absentmindedly. He was looking decidedly handsome, if a little forlorn...

"I, um..." I couldn't believe I was fumbling. My cheeks reddened. "It's a long story!"

"I, uh, think I'm going to see what's taking my Mum so long with our drinks!"

Fran stood up suddenly, and I breathed a small sigh of relief at her quick judgment of the situation. She was brash sometimes, I had to admit, but she was good at discerning the situation when she needed to.

I sat up against the sofa, watching Kevin take a seat on the armchair next to me.

"So, how have you been?" I cleared my throat, forcing confidence into my voice the best that I could. "How are you and Alana?"

He met my eye then, and I couldn't help but notice the glint of sadness in the blueish green colour of his own. I berated myself under my breath for succumbing to them. I didn't need myself falling again so soon after Justin, and especially not for a married man...

"We're going through a divorce, Suze..." he said, and I couldn't help but feel my jaw drop. "I know", he said, seeing my expression and laughing mirthlessly. "Everything's as much as a shock to me as it is to you at the moment!"

"I..." I struggled for the right words, completely at a loss at how to comfort such an old friend. "What... What happened?" I bit my lip shut. "Or shouldn't I ask?"

"No, no..." He leant forward in the chair, large hands clasped together tightly, head lowered to my mother's beige carpets in deep contemplation. "It's not like it isn't already the gossip of the town..." I stared at him, unwilling to speak until he felt like the time was right. All of a sudden, he looked up at me, and the force of his gaze stopped my heart in my chest. "The baby?" I nodded almost involuntarily, remembering the swollen bump of Alana's belly, so close to birth. "It was never even mine, Suze..."

I wasn't sure whether it was the statement itself, or the matter-of-fact tone in which Kevin spoke that was what made me gasp in horror.

"Oh, Kevin, I'm so sorry…" I felt tears spring to my eyes for him. I had always cared for Kevin, ever since we were young tearaways keeping the neighbours up until 2am. So, now, seeing his youthful face suddenly crumple into one of grief and heartbreak, was almost too much for me to bear. I stood up, making my way over to the armchair and crouching down in front of him. I took his hand, boldly, in my own. "I don't even know what to say…"

"You'd think you would know someone after two years together, you know?" he said, and his words was wrought with so much pain that I felt each one like a knife in my side. "All this time…" I heard the wobble in his voice and my heart ached. "All this time leading a double life… How could that not have eaten away at her?"

Kevin looked at me then, eyes pleading for an answer like a desperate child, and my stomach churned when thoughts of my father knocked me to the floor. I sat with my back against the armchair, legs crossed, staring out of the huge bay window opposite.

"Some people are better at hiding secrets than others, I suppose…" was all I could manage. Even Justin, I thought, with an unexpected ache in my heart, had proved that true.

"I'm glad you're home, anyway, Suze." Kevin nudged me with his leg, bringing me out of my misery and I looked up at him. In that moment, I caught a glimpse of the young boy I had grown up with all those years ago, now transformed before my eyes into a man. "At least for a little while…"

Just then, Valerie and my mother walked in with two glasses of Rose in their hands.

"Bad timing?" Valerie asked, as bold as ever. I stood up hastily, my head rushing as I did and took the wine glass from her proffered hand. "Kev, are you doing alright, sweetheart?"

Valerie sat down on the three-seater with her own glass, crossing her legs and staring at Kevin meaningfully.

I couldn't help but notice an embarrassed smile spreading across Kevin's face as he leant back in the chair. "I suppose I'm going to get this a lot now, aren't I?"

We all chuckled then at his light-hearted comment and I took a hearty sip of my Rose, hoping that Kevin Brady would stay just a little bit longer.

Chapter 8

Helen, Ireland, 2015

"I have to ask, of all the names you could have chosen, why Valerie Rice?"

I looked across at my best friend, marvelling at how well she had done for herself. I couldn't help but admire her fierce spirit.

Sally laughed, her light-hearted cackle warming my heart quite unexpectedly. It had been at least a year since we had seen each other, and even then, it had had to be under careful circumstances.

"I don't know..." she said, casually, taking a long sip of Rose. "It's got a nice ring to it, don't you think? Perfect combination of sophistication and glamour?"

I couldn't help but laugh out loud. After everything we had both been through, it seemed that nothing had changed between us. The fact of that almost brought a tear to my eye.

"They look happy, don't they?"

From where we were sat in my garden, Sally and I looked through the bay window into my kitchen. Suzy, Fran and Kevin were laughing raucously at something Graham had said and I felt my heart swell to twice its size at the simple scene.

"I'll say!" Sally emptied her glass with one, final gulp and placed it down onto the soft grass beneath the bench. "Bet you never thought you'd see this day, did you, Helen?"

My best friend's words plucked at my heart strings and I drew in a shuddering breath of unbridled joy. "Never..."

"You've done so well, hon..." I heard her say, her voice unusually quiet.

From somewhere behind us, I could hear the sound of our little pond, gurgling and rippling gently. "After everything Daniel put you through..." she halted, as if calculating the impact of her next few words, "After everything he put us both through..."

I turned to look at her then, tears brimming in my eyes and I noticed her own were slowly filling. To see Sally – a woman as hard as nails – succumb to her emotions made me want to embrace her and never let go.

"How did Suzy react when you told her?" Sally cleared her throat, fighting back her emotions. "Not well, I imagine..."

"She was shocked, to say the least", I said, laughing dryly. "But she needed to know the truth. She needed to know who her father was..." I felt my heart fill – an overflowing vat of forgotten memories. "And even now that he's gone", I brought my fingers to my lips to stem the sob that threatened, "I can't help but feel that I betrayed him!"

"No!" Sally's voice was firm and I felt her take my hand tightly in hers. She turned my chin to look at her. "Listen to me, Helen." Her green eyes, still so beautiful after all these years, took me by surprise with their urgency. "He painted you as the mother of all evil! Literally! He made that little girl in there believe you were to blame for the divorce!" I saw a tear slide down my best friend's cheek. "You see that, don't you, hon?"

I stared at her, eyes pleading with my scarred heart and my tears betrayed me.

"I know, Sally, but you don't understand!" I dabbed at my eyes with the back of my hand, my mascara transferring onto my skin in dark patches. "There were days when he would make me feel like I was the only woman in the world! He would be so kind and loving…"

"And then after that?" Sally stared at me hard, and I could almost read the words that were swimming in her eyes. "Or have you conveniently replaced all the bad memories with the good?"

I said nothing, knowing, as always, that my friend was right. Daniel had always had full control of me, even until his death.

We sat in silence for a while, and I heard Fran laughing at something Kevin had just said to Suzy. I couldn't help but notice, with a smile, that my beautiful step-daughter was blushing.

"She has his eyes, you know…" I said, finally. "Fran, I mean."

Sally glanced across at me, and I was sure I felt her body stiffen next to mine.

"Don't worry…" she said, comfortingly placing her hand in mine. "That's the only thing of Daniel's she's inherited."

I took a deep breath, blowing it out through pursed lips. "Does she know about Daniel?"

Sally stared at me then, her eyes wild, and it was as if the miserable spell we had both been under for the past ten minutes had been broken.

"Do you think I'm crazy?!"

I laughed so loud then that Graham looked out of the window of the kitchen, smiling oddly at me. I smiled back, his crooked smile still setting my heart to race after ten years together.

"I don't think I need to answer that, do I?"

I grinned across at my friend and she smacked me playfully on the arm.

"You know what I mean, missus!"

I giggled, running my hand through my curls and disentangling the knots.

"Good", I sighed, watching the giggling girls in the kitchen and feeling silently relieved at their blissful ignorance of each other's heritage. "It should stay that way, I think…"

"Helen", she said, folding her arms across her chest defiantly. "All Fran knows about her father is that he was the low-life who walked out on us after she was born." She glanced across at me, a sly look in her eyes. "Which isn't a complete lie, is it?" I smiled thinly. "So, do you think you'll ever want to tell Suzy about Fran?"

Sally's question circled over in my mind, the wheels turning constantly until I abruptly brought them to a halt.

"I must admit, I was close to telling her a couple of years ago when her and Fran first became friends." I searched the grass beneath my feet, my mind travelling back to a lazy Sunday afternoon in Foxrock. "I had rang to check up on her, see how she was doing. And then that was when she had told me that she was planning on moving to Cornwall for her job." I could feel Sally's gaze on me, drinking in my every word. "I had wanted to come down and visit her, tell her all about you and Fran. But…" I felt my heart tighten with the memory. "I could hear Daniel in the background and I, I knew it wasn't safe to ask her then."

"That's when you suggested Cornwall to Fran and I, isn't it?"

I looked at her, nodding slowly and Sally nodded back, fitting the pieces of our complicated puzzle together.

"It was the only way I could think of them meeting without Daniel being in the way. You could both move to Cornwall, start a new life away from him…" I stared at Sally, looking pensive, all of a sudden, and I placed a hand on her arm. "You don't resent me, do you, Sal? For up-hauling your life and…"

"Resent you?" She stared at me, incredulous and I couldn't help but feel a wave of affection for her. "Hon, if it hadn't been for your girl in there," she said, pointing towards the kitchen where Suzy was stood, still deep in conversation with Kevin Brady, "I don't know what would have happened to Fran and I! That man was on my tail for almost five years after Fran was born, sending me threats left, right and centre!"

Sally ran her manicured talons through her luscious hair, her eyes widening with memories of her own. "It was only when I decided to move in with my parents that he started to ease off a little..."

I watched as a small, green insect landed on her trouser leg, chuckling to myself when she flicked it off disgustedly with a gold-painted fingernail.

"We were happy and content for many years after that. We moved further north, found a little terraced house in the city and settled there until Fran went off to University. It was only two or three years later that he managed to track us down..."

She took a deep breath, puffing her large bosom out and I could see my best friend trying her best to rein in the emotions that were threatening to show themselves at any moment. "I couldn't help but laugh at the voicemail he left me..." Sally scoffed, shivering suddenly and I noticed the sky above us had begun to darken. "I could hear it in his voice. The panic and fear that his precious little girl was leaving him to start her own life in Cornwall."

She turned to me and smiled, the gesture not quite meeting her eyes. "He said he was in love with me, Helen! Can you believe him?"

I stared at her in shock, her words disabling the effort it took for me to speak.

"I know! I guess that proved to me there was more than just darkness inside that man..." I listened silently, Sally's words settling in my heart uneasily. "There was a deep, profound sickness."

"I can't believe it..." I said, forcing the words from my lips that suddenly felt dry and chapped. "All the secrets, all the..."

"Oh, Helen, I'm sorry, I shouldn't have said..."

"No, I'm sorry, Sal." I turned to her, her face still as pretty as when we were both knocking back Tequila shots in a dirty old pub in

Dublin over twenty years ago. There were only a sprinkle of laughter lines around her eyes now that hinted at her age. "If I had left him sooner, then maybe…"

"Oi!" She smacked my wrist sternly, as if I was nothing more than a child being disciplined. "Now isn't the time for maybe's and what if's!"

"True." I laughed, mirthlessly. "You're right, as always."

"You two coming in, or what?" Graham appeared in the back door, his lean frame leant casually against the doorframe. "You'll be fodder for the foxes soon, if you're not careful!"

We both chuckled and I looked up to see a dark cloud threatening over the town of Foxrock.

Picking up the pace, Sally and I made our way back to the house.

"So, what about Suzy?" Sally nudged me. "Do you think you'll ever tell her?"

"Maybe one day…" I mused, looking through the window at our beautiful daughters, "But for now, I think they're both content as they are, don't you?"

A smile spread across my best friends face. "I couldn't agree more."

Chapter 9

"Right!" Fran crouched on all fours by the TV cabinet, her pert posterior accentuated for all to see. I glanced to the doorway, where Kevin was lingering and couldn't help but notice his eyes resting on her athletic figure. When he looked back up, his eyes met mine and, immediately, I noticed him blush at being caught out. I smiled at him, surprised by the slight stab of envy I felt in my side. "Legally Blonde, or Charlie's Angels?"

Fran held up two DVD cases and we all spoke in unison.

"Charlie's Angels!"

"Alright!" Kevin rolled his eyes back towards the hallway. "I think that's my cue to leave!"

"Ah, no, Kev!" Valerie grabbed him roughly by the arm and we all laughed. "Stay and watch it with us, babe!"

I giggled as Fran opened the DVD case with a click. "You really don't have to stay if you don't want to, Kevin!"

"Ah, Suzy, don't say that to him!" Valerie looked at me with mock sadness in her pretty eyes. "How you can possibly refuse that gorgeous little face?"

Kevin grinned, shaking his head in embarrassment and I couldn't help my cheeks redden for him.

"Hey, Kev", Fran said, leaping over to the sofa and planting herself next to me in the middle. "It's fine, you can be Charlie and we'll be your angels! How about that?"

"Ha!" Valerie cackled at her daughter. "Good one, baby! How about it, Kev?"

We all stared up at him, debating whether or not to subject himself to an evening of gossip and wine. It was a lethal mix, I knew.

"Fine!" He threw his hands up in surrender and we all cheered. "I've clearly not got a say in this decision either way, have I?"

He made his way over to the only empty chair, conveniently next to me, and I felt my heart somersault inside me.

Feeling Fran nudge me gently, her eyes fixed firmly on the TV screen, I heard my mother and Valerie chatting to each other absentmindedly, a glass of wine in their hands.

"Hey, Suze?" Kevin leaned over to me, his breath in my ear. I couldn't help but notice he smelt amazing. "They *are* going to let me go by the end of the evening, aren't they?"

I giggled, taking a sip of my Rose that Fran had just refilled. "I wouldn't argue with Valerie if I were you!" I eyed him meaningfully and he grinned. "She can be quite persuasive when she wants to be!"

Kevin laughed as we turned back to the TV.

The film had started.

Author Note:

As I understand my subject matter is of a delicate and sensitive nature, I would like to make it known that all of the characters in my novel are fictional and are not based on any real-life experiences, but upon my own imagination.

Printed in Great Britain
by Amazon